A SECOND CHANCE

Alexis A. Goring

ISBN-10:1-944203-93-1
ISBN 13:978-1-944203-93-1

Endorsements

"This sweet second-chance story is sure to bring a smile to your lips as it delights your soul."~ Mary Manners, inspirational romance author

"I enjoyed this sweet story of love, forgiveness, and trusting in God's plan and purpose." ~Autumn Macarthur, USA Today bestselling author of heartwarming emotional romance.

"A Second Chance is a Hallmark-esque story for fans of inspirational romance."~ Jamie Lapeyrolerie, blogger at Books & Beverages

"A lovely story about trusting life's journey to take you to the love you deserve." ~Kelly Youngs, She Is Fierce! Founder

"A Second Chance is an inspirational story filled with a wonderful cast of characters in a novella that could easily lend itself into a series. Hopefully we'll read more from this up and coming author!" ~Mimi Milan, bestselling romance author

"A beautifully written book that takes you on the journey of two people willing to give love a second chance. Read this book and let your heart be softened and open to love however it may find you." ~Jade Callahan, LGSW

"I enjoyed reading about how a relationship can be saved by God's grace when we are willing to forgive. God can turn the greatest heartbreak into the most wonderful love story. Thank you Alexis for sharing how us humans can experience a love made in heaven."~ Alondra Martinez-Gutierrez, ACNP-BC, RNFA

ACKNOWLEDGEMENTS

First and foremost, I want to thank God for giving me the gift of writing. I am grateful to be one of His servants who work to advance His Kingdom and support the cause of Jesus Christ, His Son, through my storytelling.

Secondly, I want to praise the Lord for connecting me with my book editor Liz Tolsma. She is a God-send for me. Her knowledge of the Christian book publishing industry, compassionate heart, encouraging coaching skills, and expertise as an editor all worked together to help me to grow as a fiction writer. Working on this book with Liz took my storytelling skills to new levels of success.

I am thankful for the support of my family members: my parents who encourage me to reach for the stars, my grandmother who always prays for me and provides feedback for my stories, my brother and his wife who encourage me in my journey, and all of my extended family members. I love and appreciate every one of you. Thanks for believing in me as I pursue my dreams.

My church family is one of a kind. Thank you to my pastors, my friends, the elders, and the congregation members who supported me through the highs and lows of my publication journey. You all have a special place in my heart.

Thank you, Cynthia Hickey, for inviting me to join
your company of traditionally published authors!
You are a blessing, and this opportunity to be
published by Forget Me Not Romances is an answer
to my prayers.

My friends who endorsed this book deserve
recognition. Thank you so much! I value your time
and care. Thank you for being there for me.

Thank you to Dr. Ronda Wells for helping me with
explaining the correct medical terminologies for the
hospital scene in my story.

Finally, I want to thank my readers who waited
patiently for this second book of mine to be
published. I hope that you will enjoy it! God bless
you.

This book is dedicated to:

All the dreamers. Keep believing in your dreams
and trust God to bring His plans for you to pass in
His perfect time.

Jeremiah 29:11

Chapter 1

Knee-deep in debt from wedding expenses, Traci Hightower sighed as she filed through the credit card statements. She should be married now, back from her honeymoon in Bali, and settled into her new home with her husband.

Happy.

Not single and broke.

She slapped an envelope against the desk. Five months of struggling to survive and pay off the debt. Her meager, entry-level journalist salary didn't stretch far enough. She'd been paying her dues for seven years. She rubbed her temples. The numbers on the credit card statement blurred in front of her eyes.

The doorbell rang. A little thrill rushed through her. She stood from her cross-legged position on the floor and hopped over the mess of papers and laundry that decorated her living room. "Who is it?"

"The woman who gave you birth."

For the first time today, Traci smiled. She

opened the door and reached for a hug from the one person who never left her hanging. "Hi, Mom."

Her mom returned her daughter's embrace, then dragged her suitcase inside. She glanced around. "Oh, my."

Traci locked her door, then turned and shrugged. "I'm so glad you're here. I've been looking forward to this. Can't you stay for more than two days though?"

Mom stopped picking up the bills from the floor and faced her daughter. "No, honey. I'm sorry, but I need to return to home by Wednesday morning. Dad and I have an important meeting later that day."

Traci's heart dipped. Mom paused and placed the bills and the stack of paper she'd picked off the floor on Traci's kitchen counter. "Oh, sweetie." She cocooned her daughter in another embrace.

Traci snuggled close. She inhaled the familiar scent of her mother's favorite perfume. It smelt like coconut and lime.

"You always were a cuddler." Mom stroked her hair. "Still up to your eyeballs in debt?"

Traci nodded.

"Why don't you let me and your father help?"

Traci took a step back and made eye contact with her mom. "We've been through this. I got myself into this mess. I'll get myself out."

Mom smiled. "Your father and I were talking. We hate to see you struggling."

"You don't exactly live in a palace either. I know you want to retire soon, and I won't have you dipping into that money."

Mom reached into her purse. "Living in the nation's capital area is expensive." She rummaged through her handbag's contents. "Have you considered moving home?"

"I can't do that. I don't ever want to live anywhere else. My life and career are here."

"How's that going for you?"

Traci picked at her fingernails. "It could be better." Better boss, better pay, better office space. The works.

Mom nodded as she retrieved one sealed envelope from her purse. She looked toward Traci's kitchen. "Can we make some tea? I'd like to talk with you."

"Sure. Come with me." Traci reached for the box of peppermint tea bags and got a bottle of honey from her refrigerator. As she put the kettle on to boil, her mom settled into a wobbly kitchen chair. She smoothed the creased edges of the envelope.

Traci poured the hot water over the tea bags in each mug and the scent of peppermint filled the air. "Everything okay?"

"Just thinking, honey."

"About what?"

"Have a seat."

"Sure, just let me allow the tea to steep." After she placed a plate over each mug and set it aside, settled into the chair across from her mom. "What's up?"

"I never did like Greg."

Traci traced a ring stain on the table. "Do we have to talk about my ex-fiancé?"

"Yes, because your grandfather always trusted

my judgment."

"So, Grandpa didn't like Greg either?"

"I inherited my instincts of discernment from him. Speaking of discernment, here." She pushed the envelope within Traci's reach.

She frowned as she picked it up and tried to flatten its wrinkles. "What's this?"

"Open it. Read it, and I'll bring our tea to the table."

Traci turned over the letter-sized, manila-hued paper that was addressed to her. She drew out the paper.

Dear Traci,

If you're reading this, it means I've passed away, and your mother kept her promise to give this to you at the right time. As you know, I like to cut to the chase first and explain later. So here it is, plain and simple: I left an inheritance for you. It's enough for you to make a solid and secure living, for it will cover more than what you need for the rest of your life.

Traci dropped the letter, her hands shaking. This could be the answer to her financial struggles and give her what she always dreamed of. Her own bookstore. The thought stole her breath for a moment. She envisioned the words on the sign out front. Hallee's House. Just like she promised her cousin Hallee before she passed away from cancer. Tears welled in Traci's eyes.

Forcing herself to take a deep breath and will the emotional waterworks away, she picked the paper off the floor and continued reading.

But you cannot receive the money until after you are married, and before you are, your mother must approve of the man you want to wed. Why? Because your mother inherited my sense of judgment and discernment between right and wrong when it comes to people. She can spot someone who's going to break your heart from a mile away. I trust that you will listen to your mother now that I'm gone and can no longer advise you. So there you have it, dear. You have an inheritance. Sounds like a movie, right? Only it's not. It's better, because it's now part of the story of your life.

After you're married, you and your husband need to visit my lawyer, Chadwick Morrison. Provide him with the original copy of your marriage certificate, and he will give you your inheritance.

Your grandmother and I loved you. We wanted nothing more than for you to find the type of love that we had during our lifetime. Now, I trust that you will allow yourself to be guided by God, your mother's love, and your father's protection.

With love, your grandfather,
Henry Allen Fort

P.S. Take this seriously. Don't marry the wrong man just to get the money. Let love happen. There's no deadline. My will said you had to be married first. It didn't say when.

"Let love happen." Traci snorted as she folded the letter and placed it into the envelope. "The last time I let love happen, I was left at the altar with nothing more than a pile of bills."

Mom placed her mug on the table. "It's time for you to move on and trust God."

"I trusted God to bring me a husband. He brought me Greg. Remember? The man who left me on my wedding day and ran off with my best friend?"

"Honey, I know it hurts, but that was months ago. You shouldn't allow Greg's actions and wayward heart to tarnish your future. Be glad he showed you his true colors before tying the knot. Honestly, look at this as a blessing. God protected you from a lifetime of heartache."

Traci focused on her I Love Maryland mug.

Mom touched her hand. "Your grandfather just wanted to see you happy in a committed romantic relationship like he and your grandma had. Like your father and I have."

Traci sipped her tea.

"Keep the letter." Mrs. Hightower pushed her chair back. "Do you want me to stay here or at a hotel?"

"Here, Mom, of course. You can stay in my room. I'll sleep on the couch."

"Alright then. I'm going to put my luggage in your room. After that, we'll clean your apartment."

Traci picked up the mugs while her mind ran a marathon. Forgive her ex-fiancé and move on?

Trust God?
Impossible.

Chapter 2

"How'd it go, covering the farmers' market?"

Traci clutched her chest. "Would you please stop scaring me?" She swiveled around in her rolling office chair and glared at Carla Simmons, her colleague at the *Maryland Times* newspaper.

Carla smirked. "Are you always this happy to see me?"

Traci spun around to face her computer. "Delighted." Maybe her monotone answer would get rid of her coworker.

"Good. Because I have some great news for you. We're going out tonight." Carla's naturally curly, raven-black hair bounced as she nodded, and her caramel complexion glowed.

"We? As in you and me?"

"Yes. It's time you got out again. You've got to meet new men."

Did Carla know about the letter? The money? No, Traci hadn't told anyone, so there was no correlation, right? Of course not.

"Why do you say that?" She continued typing her story.

Carla spun Traci's chair so they would be face-to-face. "Because hun, I want to see you happy again."

"Happy? I'm happier than a sugar addict at a bakery."

"No, you're not. Not since Greg left you."

Traci's bottom lip quivered, and she balled her fists.

"Traci, we, your colleagues, your friends, care about you, and we want to see you find a man who's worthy of your time and affection. You can't keep burying your emotions by working all day and night. You need to deal with the breakup and meet new men. Get out there, girl. You're a good catch."

Then, why did Greg leave her at the altar?

"So, what do you say?"

Traci stared at the buttons on Carla's red blouse. "Say about what?"

"Are you going out on the town with me tonight?"

"I don't know. I'm not ready."

"Okay, then." Carla blew out a breath. "Maybe next time."

"Don't count on it." Traci turned to her computer, muttering.

"I heard that."

She was almost finished with the farmers' market story when the calendar alert flashed across the screen of her cell phone. She just about jumped out of her chair. She forgot she needed to cover the opening of the new upscale restaurant in Baltimore,

Marie Claire's.

She glanced at the time on her computer screen. Only five. If she left work now, she could go home, change into more glamorous clothes, and make it to the restaurant in time for their grand opening at seven.

Maybe she should have brought Carla along.

No, she would have wanted to hook her up with the first cute waiter they saw.

~

Traci smoothed the silk fabric of her little black dress. Her hands glided over the material as she checked it for any creases, smoothing it to perfection. She reached for her pearls, a gift from her dad when she graduated from college.

"Always remember, you are my princess." His eyes shone when she opened the gift. "And you deserve a prince."

"You'll always be my princess." Greg used those same words to woo her when they were dating. "And I, as your prince, will protect, love, and cherish you forever."

Apparently, forever had an expiration date. He left her at the altar and shattered her heart.

She straightened. Greg was in the past. He was not her real prince. Not even a real gentleman. She was better off without him. One day, she would meet someone who would ruin her lipstick, not her mascara.

She applied her favorite rose-pink lip gloss, eyeliner, and mascara. Professional but flirty. Perfect for a night out on the town. She swept her unruly hair into a bun and slipped her feet into a pair of black pumps.

She observed the tight bun in her vanity mirror. Too professional. It might be a better idea to let her hair down, at least for tonight. After all, this was a five-star restaurant.

For whatever the reason, she had this urge to dress to the nines.

Not that she was husband hunting.

That was the last thing she was doing.

~

Marc Roberts pulled up to the new five-star restaurant and handed his car keys to the valet. "Thanks, man."

The tuxedo-clad valet nodded and slid into the driver's seat, then sped off. Marc did a double-take, holding his breath until he was sure the man didn't crash his vehicle.

The doorman smiled at Marc and opened the entrance door, ushering him in with a gesture. Marc nodded his head and walked in, where the maître d' greeted him.

"Dining alone?"

Marc nodded. He hated sitting at a table for one. But as someone who found himself being single more often than in a relationship, he'd gotten used to it.

"Follow me."

As Marc walked into the restaurant's dining area, he bumped into a table. The water glass on it tilted and spilled onto the white cloth.

The table's occupant gasped. He turned to her. Correction. The table's gorgeous occupant gasped.

"I'm so sorry, ma'am." Was he flushed?

Her beautiful, hazel-green eyes arrested him. His heart flopped like a bunny.

She offered him a timid smile. "That's no problem." She grabbed a notebook and pen from the path of the water.

He cleared his throat, willing his voice to work. "Are you a restaurant critic or something?"

The woman turned her head just a little bit. "Yes, I am."

"Enjoy your dinner. Sorry again about the water." The maître d' escorted him to a table only a few rows away from the gorgeous lady reporter.

He settled into his cushioned chair and perused the extensive menu. From the sound of it, the restaurant might live up to the billing it got in the magazine he read.

"What can I get you to drink? We have a lovely merlot, chardonnay, or our finest red wine."

"Just water."

"Very well. Would you like time to look at the menu, or are you ready for me to take your order?"

"Yes, I'll have the tomato bisque, the blackened salmon, and the ratatouille."

The waitress nodded as she scribbled Marc's order onto her notepad before disappearing into the kitchen.

While he waited for his food, he surveyed the restaurant, taking in the scenery, ambiance, and soft instrumental music. He stopped at the sight of the beautiful woman whom he had bumped into earlier.

He'd never seen anyone so stunning. She wore a sleek black dress, pearls, and just a touch of makeup. But it was her honey blonde hair that tumbled down her back that captivated his attention.

He couldn't breathe.

She wrote something in her notebook. Did she like her meal? She smiled at her waiter, nodded, and laughed. She must have.

He'd bet his dinner she had a heart of gold.

"Here you are, sir." Marc's waitress placed the steamy bowl of bisque on the table in front of him. "Can I get you anything else?"

Yes, her number.

He gazed at the woman seated several tables away. An idea struck him. "Yes, can you do me a favor?" He leaned in and whispered to his waitress. She scurried off. He grinned as he thought of all the possibilities that could come from the carrying out of his genius idea. He forced himself to eat.

If he kept staring at the woman at the other table, there might be a problem.

~

Traci penned a few final words onto her notepad, closing thoughts for her story on the restaurant's grand opening. She was so focused and inspired tonight by the ambiance, atmosphere, and stellar service of the wait staff, she completed an entire first draft of the feature story within forty minutes of being there.

Something struck her about the place. Maybe it was the soft lighting, the piano music, and the quiet clink of forks against fine china. Whatever it was, it stirred buried thoughts of romance.

She pushed them aside.

Now came her least favorite time of the night. She closed her reporter's notebook and reached for her purse. Paying the bill for her expensive food. At least the paper would reimburse her for the outlay.

As her waiter stopped at her table to collect her now-empty plates, she asked him for the check.

"Your meal was paid for, miss."

She froze as she reached for her much-used credit card. "What?"

"Your meal," the waiter slowed his speech, "was paid for in full."

"Paid for in full?"

"Yes, ma'am."

"By whom?"

The waiter pointed. "The gentleman a few tables down."

Traci dared to glance that way. A very handsome gentleman smiled at her. Her face warmed. It was the same man who bumped into her table earlier that night and spilled her water. A mature air hung around the man with coffee-brown eyes, an award-winning smile, and a look that made women want to get to know him.

Was he as kind as he was handsome?

Traci had learned her lesson with Greg. Never judge a man by his outward appearance, no matter how good-looking he was. She wanted to see past a man's looks to his personality and heart, because that's what mattered most.

But goodness knows, she'd like a man who was as handsome as he was compassionate.

She caught herself staring. Woops. With effort, she pulled her attention back to the waiter. "I don't know what to say."

"A simple thank you should do." He handed her

a business card. "He wanted you to have this." He turned to leave.

She grabbed his arm. "Wait." She reached into her purse and retrieved her business card and a pen and wrote, "Thank you" on the back it. She bit the pen cap. Should she ask him to call her? No. Leave that action up to him.

"Give him my card please. And thank you so much for the excellent service. Please, tell the chef the meal was delicious."

The waiter smiled, nodded, and proceeded to her admirer. She snatched her belongings and left the restaurant, not waiting to see the man's reaction when he received her business card.

No point in appearing desperate.

Chapter 3

Marc bounced his white, baseball-size stress ball off the left wall of his cubicle in the newspaper office where he worked his beat as a politics reporter. For now. Until he could get back to Chicago and work for the *Reporter.*

He thought of her. Traci. His dream girl. From the restaurant. Now, all he needed to do was to get up the nerve to call her. He retrieved her business card from his wallet and stared at it.

"What's that, bro?"

Marc knew that voice. His friend and colleague, Victor Hall. Marc shoved Traci's business card underneath his keyboard. "Nothing."

Victor ignored Marc's comment, reached over Marc, and maneuvered the business card from under the keyboard. "'Traci Hightower, food critic and education reporter for the *Maryland Times*.' What's this about?"

Marc snatched it from him. "None of your business."

Victor's eyes widened. "You met her, didn't you?"

Marc grinned. "Yeah. She was reviewing Marie Claire's."

"So, what are you going to do?"

"Nothing. Yet."

Victor scrunched his eyebrows. "Why?"

Marc sighed. "Candi dumped me last weekend. She said she just wants to be friends."

Victor crossed his arms and leaned against the left wall of Marc's cubicle. "Was this before or after you met Traci?"

"Before."

Victor slapped his thighs. "Well then, looks like God was watching out for you. The wrong girl dumped you a few days before He brought the right girl into your life. You better move on it."

Marc squeezed the ball. "I can't."

"Why not?"

"What if she just wants to be friends? Like all the rest of my ex-girlfriends?"

Victor grabbed Traci's business card from beside Marc's keyboard. "Well, you'll never know if you don't go on at least one date with your dream girl, now will you?"

Victor whipped out his cell phone.

Marc just about jumped out of his chair, but didn't want to distract his colleagues. Instead, he hissed at his colleague in a low tone. "What are you doing?"

Victor's eyes twinkled as he gave Marc a knowing look. "I'm making you a date with destiny."

Marc stood and swiped for the phone. "Don't." But Victor was already leaving a voice mail. Marc slumped in his chair.

"Hey Traci, this is Victor. I am calling on behalf of my colleague, Marc. He'd like to talk to you. Would you please call him at this number?"

Marc rubbed his temples as Victor recited the digits to Marc's personal cell phone.

His friend ended the call and returned the business card to Marc. "All done. Your future is in motion. The follow-through is up to you."

Marc shook his head, then looked up at his friend. "I want to be mad at you right now but . . ."

"You can thank me when she says, 'I do.'" Victor flashed a mischievous grin. "I've got a good feeling about this one."

~

Marc strolled up the flower-lined path toward his sister Gina Braxton's townhouse. He promised to babysit her kids tonight so that she could meet her latest book deadline. He approached the front door and rang the bell, the pitter-patter of little feet and excited voices of his niece and nephew emanating from inside. After what sounded like a struggle of grunts and giggles, the front door swung open.

"Uncle Marky!" Samantha and Regan greeted in unison.

Marc stepped into the foyer and scooped his niece and nephew into his arms. "How are my favorite munchkins?" He gave each of them a kiss.

"Good," Samantha replied.

Marc returned the kids to a standing position on the floor. His niece gazed him with a smile that reached her eyes, but Regan sucked his thumb and held onto Marc's left leg. "Mommy sad," he said.

"Where is your Mom?" Marc locked the front door.

Samantha leaned against his right side and hugged his waist. "She's in her room. Crying."

He ruffled his niece's hair. "Who wants to play hide-and-seek?"

They answered together. "Me!"

"You two go hide, and I'll check on your Mom. Then I'll find you."

Samantha and Regan ran to find their favorite hiding places inside the house. He made his way up the stairs to the master bedroom, his heart aching for his sister.

The door was shut, but Gina's weeping reached his ears as he approached. He knocked. "Gina?"

She didn't answer, but her crying softened.

"I'm coming in." He opened the door, which, to his relief, was unlocked.

She lay curled in a fetal position on top of her bed with tissues and five empty boxes strewn everywhere. He sat next to her, her face buried in her pillows.

"Gina." He touched her left shoulder.

His sister, her back to him, shook him off. "Leave me alone."

"Please, look at me."

"I said leave me alone."

"You can't go on like this. It's been a year. Let me help you find someone to talk to."

She sat up, her eyes puffy and red, dark half-moons under them. Somehow, she still managed to glare at him. "I'm not crazy. I don't need a shrink."

"I don't think you're crazy. But I do think you need to talk to someone who understands and can help you heal."

Her bottom lip quivered and tears rushed down her face. "No one understands. Jimmy . . . he's . . . gone." She shuddered.

"Maybe other firefighter wives who have lost their husbands in the line of duty." He handed her a tissue. She took it and blew her nose. He drew her into a hug. Her tears soaked his shirt sleeves. "We'll see him one day when Jesus comes to take us home to heaven."

"I want him now. I can't live without my husband. The only man I've loved. I'm a horrible mother without him." Her tears fell again.

Marc just held his sister and let her weep. How did he help her?

Dear God, please heal Gina's pain. You laid the love of her life to rest. But we know that gone is not forever in your book. If Gina continues to follow you, she'll see her husband again when you return. I know that there are no words I can say to help my sister in her grief. So Lord, please, intervene and show me what to do too.

Without warning, her sobbing stopped. She pushed away from him and glanced toward her bedroom door.

"Where are my kids?"

He managed a small smile. "They're waiting for me to find them. We're playing hide-and-seek."

She frowned. "Oh."

He touched her knee. "I'm here for you, sis.

Always."

"I know."

"Do you still have to meet your book deadline tonight?"

She nodded.

"Is there food in the pantry?"

She nodded again.

"Would you like for me to fix dinner for your kids and get them ready for bed?"

Her eyes glistened. "Would you?"

"Anything for you, sis."

She gave him a hug. "I don't know what I'd do without you. I'm glad you're my brother."

He squeezed her. "And I'm glad you're my sister."

"Uncle Marky!" Samantha's called from downstairs. "Come find us!"

"Yeah!" Regan echoed Samantha's request.

Gina chuckled the smallest of bits. "You better go. I'm feeling better. Don't worry about me."

Marc rose and started for the door, but turned around for a moment to assure his sister. "Everything's going to be okay. God's got this."

She wiped her eyes and picked up the tissues from the floor. He shut the door behind himself. As he reached the bottom of the stairs, he sent up one more silent prayer. *I trust you Lord. Please help Gina to trust you too. We know you never leave us. Draw Gina close to you and heal her broken heart.*

Samantha hollered. "Uncle Marky, we're getting tired of hiding."

"Well, that's too bad, because I'm about to find you."

The kids giggled before bursting out of their hiding spaces behind the couch. "You found us."

Marc reached out and tickled the kids. He swung Regan around in a circle. "I'm hungry. Are you hungry?"

"Yes." Samantha hopped on one foot.

"Well then, who wants to help me make dinner?"

"I will." Regan rushed to the kitchen.

Marc crouched in a runner's starting position. "Last one to the kitchen has to wash the dishes."

Samantha sprinted ahead of him. He didn't mind dish duty. Most of all, he didn't mind babysitting Gina's kids. One day, maybe he would be so lucky to find true love, settle down, and start a family of his own.

Traci's image flashed across his mind, and his heart warmed. Perhaps that day would come sooner than he thought.

Chapter 4

Marc stretched his limbs as he woke up, stiff from a night on Gina's couch. No sunshine peeked through the blinds, though a light shone from the kitchen. "What time is it?"

"Just after five." Gina came from the kitchen holding a breakfast tray complete with scrambled tofu eggs, vegetarian sausage, toast, a glass of orange juice, and a bottle of water. She set the tray on the end table next to him. "Sorry, didn't mean to scare you."

"What are you doing up so early?"

"You told me to wake you at five, remember?"

He yawned and completed his stretch. "Thanks for letting me crash here." He eyed the food and savored the sweet aroma. "And you fixed me breakfast."

"Anytime." She grabbed a cup of coffee and sat in the chair across from him. "So, what's going on?"

"What do you mean?" He forked a pile of the

eggs into his mouth.

"How is work? Dating? Life?"

Marc nearly choked. He paused to finish chewing and swallowing, then gulped down his entire glass of orange juice. "It's going great, sis. Better than I hoped."

Gina raised an eyebrow.

"No." He stabbed a vegetarian sausage link with his fork. "I'm not telling you anything."

Her eyes twinkled. "You met a girl. But not just any girl. She must be pretty special if she makes you grin from ear-to-ear like you are."

He almost choked on his food again. This time he reached for his glass of water and gulped it. "Your investigative drills are hazardous to my health."

She sipped her coffee without taking her gaze from him. After avoiding her scrutiny, Marc sat back and sighed. "Okay, what do you want to know?"

She set her cup on the table and sat pretzel style. "Everything. What does she look like? Where does she work? How did you meet? What do you like about her?"

"Beautiful. *Maryland Times* newspaper. Marie Claire's restaurant. And everything."

Gina clapped. After a moment, she sobered. "Just be careful."

"Whoa, did you see the weather change? We went from sunny days to forecasting rain."

"I am happy for you. Delighted, truly, but I want you to be cautious. You get your hopes up so high only to see them come crashing down when the girl you like dumps you and runs off with some other guy."

"I'm aware of that."

"Good." She leaned over and rubbed the top of his hand. "I love you and don't want to see you get hurt. Again."

He glanced at his watch. "I need to go to work. Thanks for breakfast. Tell your kids bye for me."

"You're welcome, and I will." Gina stood and hugged him.

"I'm here for you. Always, okay?"

"Right back at you."

Gina followed him to the front door. "Have a good day at work."

Marc just kept walking and waved to signal thank you and goodbye all at once. How wonderful it would be to have a wife telling him that every day.

~

Traci tapped her blue pen on her reporter's notebook as her focus turned from the meeting in the newsroom to her inheritance.

How much money was it? It would be nice to hire a personal chef to fix all of her meals. Only question was, where did she find a nice man to marry?

"Ms. Hightower." Her boss's voice interrupted her thoughts.

Traci straightened and focused her full attention on Calvin and on her colleagues around the large, dark wood table. "Yes, sir?"

"Stories." Her boss clipped his words. "What stories are you working on for this week's newspaper?"

"Oh yes." She flipped through her notepad. "Stories."

After turning a few pages of notes and old story assignments, she found her most current list of ideas. "I'd like to write a back-to-school preview for our county's public schools. And I'd like to cover a few back-to-school fairs in August, kind of a blitz."

Her boss nodded. "Sounds good. But I won't need that for a few weeks. Give me something I can use now."

"Sure." She racked her brain for anything happening this week. Inheritance. Money. No.

After a full ten seconds of silence, Carla spoke. "There's a new soup kitchen in South Bowie. I can't cover opening day because of another assignment I have, but if Traci could go in my place, maybe that would be good."

The manager glanced from Carla to Traci and back again, back and forth like he was watching a tennis match. "Very well. I want that story on my desk by noon on Tuesday."

"Um, boss?" Carla waved her pen. "The grand opening is tonight."

"I want that story on my desk by noon tomorrow, Ms. Hightower. Is that clear?"

"Yes, sir."

"Good." Calvin gathered his papers. "Meeting adjourned. Everyone return to work."

Traci waited for Carla as everyone else, including Calvin, filed out of the conference room. "Thanks for sharing your story idea with me."

"You're welcome." Carla picked up her notebook and purse.

"Would you please send your notes on the soup kitchen's grand opening to me as soon as you have time today?"

"Sure, girl. But first, I want to know what's going on."

Traci leaned back. "What do you mean?"

"Honey, you have not been the same since Greg dumped you, but these past few weeks, you've taken it to a whole other level."

Traci crossed her arms and tipped her head to the left. Carla mocked her gesture and raised her eyebrows. After a five second stare down, Traci uncrossed her arms, straightened her head, and sighed. "Fine."

"Fine?"

Traci pivoted around to make sure that she and Carla were the only ones in or near the conference room. She shut the door. "Promise me you won't tell a soul."

"I won't unless you've done something wrong. Then we may have to get the police involved."

"Carla!"

"Girl, I'm just kidding. You wouldn't harm anyone." Traci settled in the seat next to Carla, who turned her chair to face Traci. "Well?"

She let out a low breath and told her friend about the inheritance money, her grandfather's stipulations concerning her cashing the inheritance, her Mom's intuition about the guys in Traci's life, and the tale of how she met Marc. "So, that's my story." She pulled Marc's business card from her purse and handed it to Carla.

She stared at Traci. "Wow."

"I know, right? So much to take in."

"No. So much to do and plan."

Traci gave Carla a wary expression. "Like what?"

She grabbed Traci's phone, squinted at the business card, and started dialing, then placed her hand over the receiver. "Like your wedding."

Traci opened her mouth. She reached to snatch the phone from Carla's grasp.

"No! Don't call him."

But Carla stood, walked away, and spoke. "Good morning, this is Carla from the *Maryland Times*. I am calling on behalf of my colleague, Ms. Traci Hightower. She is working on a story that involves your colleague, Marc Roberts, and she needs to talk to him at his earliest convenience today. Please have him call her at this number."

Traci stood across from her matchmaker friend, shooting glares at her. Carla continued, unfazed. "Thank you, and have a lovely day."

Chapter 5

Traci stared out the window and wished she was carefree, strolling the streets of Paris and dining at the popular cafés instead of stuck in her office cubicle, working on meeting a deadline.

She glanced at the clock. Seven. If finished typing her notes into the computer, it would only take her about ten minutes to write the story, and she could be out of here by eight. The office was so silent that if she dropped a pin, she was sure she'd hear it hit the floor. She pulled up some music on her phone to fill the void. To help her forget she was alone.

She was tasked with writing another restaurant review, this time of a small French café that opened in Crofton. The food was okay, but her dining experience was nothing like it was at Marie Claire's. The fare was tasty but not satisfying. The music was too loud, the painted walls too dull, and the wait staff too casual. It took every last professional skill of hers to not write a negative report of this new place.

Who was she kidding? That café was terrible.

As she typed her notes, Marc's face flashed across the movie screen of her mind. Heat rose in her cheeks, and for a moment, she was glad her colleagues in the next two cubicles were not here to notice it. But her face cooled. One full week later, he hadn't called her. No man took that long to phone if he was interested in a woman. He was a dream of the past.

Time for her to let go of what could have been.

Just as she finished typing the last word of her ten pages of notes, her phone rang.

She ignored it for a while and focused on writing the lead to her story, but by the third time through her ringtone, she was too annoyed to focus. "Who is this?"

"Hey, is this Traci?"

"Yes. Who is this? I'm on deadline."

"Oh, I'm sorry. Maybe I should call another time."

His kind tone stabbed at her. She'd been rude. She softened her voice. "I apologize. I'm on deadline, but I have a few minutes. Who is this?"

"Marc Roberts."

Her heart dropped. Of all the times to give in to rudeness.

"Hello?"

Traci smiled and hoped the sentiment would carry through the phone. "Yes, Marc. How are you?"

"I'm doing pretty well. How about you?"

A smile tugged at the corner of her lips. She was

talking to him. And taking too much time to answer. "I'm on deadline."

There was a brief pause. "Oh, right. We can talk another time. I understand time crunches."

"No," she blurted. "I mean, we can talk for a minute. I could use a break."

"The message your colleague left said I should call you because you needed to talk to me about a story you're working on?"

"Marie Claire's?"

"I'm not sure."

"Oh yes, that story." When Carla called him, she said that Traci needed to talk with him about an article. However, she had already submitted that piece.

"You know, I have everything I need. But thank you for calling." Oh no. She just ended the conversation. She didn't want him to hang up yet. Think, think, think.

"Oh well, okay then."

"Lunch."

"What?"

"Let's meet up for lunch." The warmth in her face returned. Thank goodness he wasn't here.

"I'd love to meet you."

Her hand holding the phone trembled. "I'd like that. A lot."

"Can we get together tomorrow? I know it's Friday, and you're probably getting ready for the weekend but—"

"I'd love to."

"Great. Where?"

She shared the location of her favorite bistro not

far from where she worked. They exchanged pleasantries and ended the phone call.

Could this be the start of something beautiful?

~

Traci pushed a wisp of her hair out of her face for the fifth time in five minutes. She glanced at her watch. Marc was fifteen minutes late to their date. Fifteen minutes. Was this a sign?

Just as she started to change her mind and walk out of the bistro, he entered. And smiled. Her heart fluttered. She waved and settled back into her seat.

"Hi there." He reached out for a hug.

She eased into his light embrace, returning the hug, then sat back.

"It's so good to meet you in person, and at this bistro, of all places."

"Of all places?"

He slid into the seat across the table. "This is my sister's favorite place to bring her children. The owner lets kids eat free during lunch hours on the weekends. They love it here."

"That's nice." She picked up the menu. "What does your sister do for a living?"

"She's an author."

"What does she write?"

Marc scrolled through his phone. "Hold on. I always have to check my notes to make sure I say it right."

She laughed. "It's that serious?"

He nodded. "Gina writes award-winning inspirational romance that encourages the hearts of women."

"Sounds like something I need to read." She

warmed at her unintended admission.

His eyes widened.

"I mean, I'd love to read her books, they sound delightful. Inspirational romance. What does that term mean?"

"I have an answer written down for that too. Hold on." He played with his phone. "Inspirational romance is a subgenre of fiction that infuses religion and draws a spiritual thread through the story in the lives of the characters."

Traci returned her gaze to her list of meal choices. "Oh."

Marc put his phone away and picked up his copy of the menu. "Not a fan?"

"Oh, I'm sure that your sister is a great writer."

"I take it that inspirational romance is not your cup of tea?"

Traci shrugged. "You could say that."

Marc leaned in and wiggled his eyebrows. "Promise me that you won't tell Gina that."

Traci chuckled. "Don't worry, I won't."

After they studied their menus for a while, a waiter approached their table and cleared his throat. "Good afternoon. My name is Walter, and I'll be your waiter today."

She placed her order of kale salad with grapes and diced apples. He ordered a half-chicken and potatoes. They both ordered a bottle of water.

"Hungry?" She hadn't missed his lean build when he entered the restaurant.

"Always."

"First date I've been on when the guy orders dinner for lunch." She wanted to crawl under the table. Why had she said that? "Not that this is a date."

He reached across the table and touched her hands. "I'd love to call this our first date if you will."

She now understood what the word swoon meant. "I'd like that. A lot."

"Me too."

They chatted about work until their food arrived. They bowed their heads and said a silent blessing before digging in.

Marc stabbed at a piece of white meat. "So, since this is our first date, I'd like to know something."

"Sure. What would you like to know?"

"What are you looking for in a relationship?"

She moved a few apple chunks around on her dish. How should she answer without sounding too forward? What did he expect? "Someone like you." She didn't dare peek at him but kept her focus on her square, yellow plate.

Whew. He didn't laugh. She glanced up as he dumped sour cream on his potato.

"What are you looking for in a relationship?"

"Besides someone like you?" Marc's tone was light.

They needed to turn up the air conditioning in this place. "How sweet, but you know . . . I mean . . . like traits. What are your deal breakers?"

Marc sipped his water. "Honestly?"

She nodded, her mouth full of food.

"Honesty." The omnipresent smile left his face.

She swallowed hard. "I figure there's a story behind that. Care to share?"

Marc sighed, finger-combing his thick hair. He leaned in.

"I've been played. Lied to, and most frequently, dumped by women who want to just be friends."

She guzzled her water.

He leaned back. "I believe that honesty is the best policy in any relationship. No secrets that could rock your partner's world, you know?"

She gripped her fork and concentrated on her nearly-gone salad. The inheritance. What should she do? She couldn't tell him she had a secret. A secret that would rock his world for sure, if they fell in love. One that could be a deal breaker.

She didn't want to lose him just as she got to know him. And, it wasn't like they were about to get married. Surely, it wouldn't hurt their budding relationship if she kept it from him, at least for now.

"Traci?"

She startled and dropped her fork on the floor. "I agree. Honesty is the best policy."

Just not right now.

Chapter 6

Marc paced in the hospital lobby, the glare of the fluorescent lights bouncing off his phone as he stared at the text message that brought him here. The one from Gina that made him put down the carrot he was peeling, grab his keys, and rush over. "On my way to the hospital. Kids and I were in an accident. Kids are fine. I only have a few injuries."

So, here he sat, in the uncomfortable chair with the itchy fabric and wooden arm rests.

The door to the ER slid opened. A nurse holding a clipboard emerged. "Marc Roberts?"

"Yes."

"Here for first name Gina?"

"She's my sister."

"Follow me."

He trailed after the nurse through the doors, down a corridor, his tennis shoes squeaking on the shiny floors. She led him into an area where sky-blue curtains hid ER rooms. She stopped and whipped the curtain to the side.

His sister sat on the hospital bed with a tan fabric wrap over her left wrist and a wrap over her left leg. His gut twisted.

She flashed him a lopsided smile. "Hey, bro. Thanks for coming by."

His stomach relaxed a little as he pecked her on the cheek. "I'm so glad you're okay."

"The doctor gave her morphine to help with the pain. We have to admit her tonight to because her left leg suffered a dirty open fracture, which means her bone was sticking out through her skin and that her open wound became unclean from the car wreck. But we can fix that in surgery."

He let out a low blow of breath. "Sounds like a lot to handle. What happens next?"

The doctor stepped in before the nurse could answer. He shook Marc's hand. "Good evening, sir. My name is Dr. Karl Richardson. I'll be overseeing Gina's care. And you are?"

"Marc Roberts. I'm Gina's brother."

The doctor nodded. "Any questions for me?"

"Yes. When will my sister recover and be discharged?"

"Well, that depends. She could go home in a few days. After the cast comes off her leg, she'll have to do physical therapy because her bones have to be immobilized in order to heal and knit back together. She should be back to one hundred percent by the new year, but we'll see."

Marc squeezed Gina's shoulder. "It may take time, but you'll be okay, sis."

The nurse checked Gina's blood pressure. "Yes, she will be okay, but we need to keep her here for a couple of days. She'll have surgery this evening."

Gina stared at the nurse with glazed eyes. "I can't stay here." She dragged out her words. Probably from the morphine. "My kids . . ."

"Don't worry about Regan and Samantha." Marc rubbed her upper arm. "I'll take them home."

"But you don't have the key. And work . . ."

"Don't worry about it. That's what family is for."

Gina's eyes welled with tears. "If Jimmy were alive, we wouldn't need . . ."

"I know. But it's what I'm here for. I'll work it out. Just take care of yourself, okay?"

"Bring the kids to say goodnight." Gina's eyes drooped.

Marc turned to the nurse. "Where are my sister's kids?"

"They're in the next room. The doctor was just looking them over."

"Are they okay?"

"Yes." Gina spoke up before the nurse could answer. "God took care of us. Like always."

The nurse motioned to Marc. "Come with me."

He followed her to the next room. Regan and Samantha rushed to him, each holding onto one of his tailored-trouser covered legs.

"Uncle Marky!" A torrent of tears poured from their eyes.

Why did they have to go through this? He reached down and engulfed them in a bear hug. "It's going to be okay."

"A car hit us. Mommy got hurt." Regan sucked his thumb.

"Yes, your mommy is hurt, but she will be as

good as new. And you will be fine too."

Someone nearby cleared their throat. He looked up to see Dr. Richardson.

"Hello again, Marc. Any questions for me about Gina's kids?"

Marc stood and faced the doctor while the kids clung to his legs. "Were they injured? I don't see any bruises."

"No. They were lucky. Left the accident without a mark or a scratch. The CAT scans showed no brain injury in either child. However, I recommend you follow up with an appointment with their primary care physician."

"Thanks."

"And we'll need to see and verify your ID before you leave with the children. My nurse, Kelli, can help you with that procedure."

After verifying his ID and taking his nephew and niece to say good night to their mom, Marc helped the sleepy kids into his car. No sooner than settling into their seats, the kids were asleep. He gazed at their peaceful, angelic faces.

What would life be like if he were married and had a few kids of his own? Traci's beautiful face came to mind. He'd been busy covering story assignments and meeting deadlines. He planned to call her tonight while his dinner was cooking, but now it was too late.

Would she forgive him for not calling in two weeks?

~

"Good night Uncle Marky," Samantha whispered as she drifted off to sleep.

Marc tucked his sleeping niece in bed with her princess-pink quilt. "Good night, sweetheart." He turned off the ceiling light.

Next, he went to check on Regan, who to his surprise, sat in bed clutching his teddy bear for dear life.

"What's wrong buddy?" Marc plopped on the foot of his bed.

"I miss mommy." A torrent of tears rolled down his cheeks.

Marc cradled his nephew. All of this had to be so hard on him. "Hey buddy, it's okay. Your mommy should be home soon."

Regan pulled away. "Tomorrow?"

Marc tousled his nephew's hair. "Sooner than you think."

"Okay." Regan gave his thumb a good suck before talking around it. "Read me a story?"

"Sure, buddy. What do you want to hear?"

"*Puppy, Come Home.*"

Marc resisted the urge to laugh. "Sure, where is it?"

Regan, still sucking his thumb, pointed toward his bookcase. After tucking Regan underneath his sports-car-decorated bed covers, Marc sat next to his nephew, opened the book *Puppy Come Home,* and began to read.

Five minutes later, Regan was fast asleep, and Marc was yawning.

"Good night, buddy." He returned the book to the shelf and turned off the lights.

He found his way to the guest room and fell on top of the bed. All he wanted to do was to go to sleep.

He had to make time to call Traci tomorrow. Before she drifted out of his life.

Chapter 7

"Earth to Traci."

Carla's words pulled Traci out of her deep thoughts. The clink of silverware against plates, the aroma of tacos and hamburgers, the warmth of the Sunday afternoon sun came back into focus.

"What's going on girl?" Carla, seated in the booth across from her, cradled her coffee cup.

Traci sighed. "I don't want to tell Marc about the inheritance." They'd had a few dates, but now he hadn't called her in a week.

Carla tsk-tsked. "Yes, but you know you need to before things get serious."

"I know."

"You know that if you tell him, you run the risk of losing him. Right?"

"I know."

"But it's better to tell him than wait for him to find out for himself." Carla bit into her sandwich.

"That's impossible. Only three people know about the inheritance. Four, really. My Mom, my family lawyer, me, and you." Traci narrowed her eyes. "You don't plan on saying anything, do you?"

Carla gasped. "Me? No, girlfriend. That's your place, not mine. I've never even met him, remember?"

Traci poked the lettuce of her fruit-topped salad. Carla was right. But was it worth the risk?

"Okay, change of topic. Why don't we go visit the bookstore? Unless you have other plans for the rest of your Sunday?"

Traci threw her napkin on the table. "I love the bookstore."

"I know, and it's the perfect place to get your mind off of you know, that secret."

"I agree."

"You should probably finish your lunch first." Carla reached for her half-empty bottle of green smoothie. "You need to eat."

"I'm not starving myself."

"Just saying. You've been thinking about that secret of yours, and it shows. You don't eat much when you're stressed."

"Fine. I'll finish, so we can go."

But the secret gnawed at her more than hunger pains.

~

Traci and Carla walked through the double door entrance to the bookstore. The scent of green tea and muffins greeted them.

"Oh, my. Do you smell that?"

"I sure do."

"Another reason why I love this bookstore. Excuse me while I go follow my dreams." Carla scooted off in the direction of the café.

"Where are you going?"

She stopped and faced Traci. "To get a muffin or a cupcake or whatever else smells good."

"But we just ate lunch."

"I didn't have dessert. It's overdue. I'll look for you after I satisfy my sweet tooth."

Traci chuckled. "Okay. I'll be browsing the book shelves."

Carla made a beeline for the other side of the store while Traci strolled toward the Christian fiction section. Marc told her that his sister was a bestselling author. Could she find Gina's book? She frowned. It would help if she knew her last name.

She could text Marc. Sure, because he hadn't called her in two weeks. He'd think she was forward. Maybe he didn't like her. Maybe he wanted to let her down without hurting her.

But then again, what did she have to lose?

An inheritance.

Before she chickened out, she whipped out her phone and sent him a text. "Hey! I'm at the bookstore. Would love to read one of your sister's books. What's her last name?"

Moments later, her phone buzzed with his reply. "You're at the bookstore? Which one?"

Traci placed the self-help book she'd been flipping through underneath her arm. "The one in Bowie. Why?"

She almost dropped the book when she read Marc's reply. "I'm here, too, with my sister's kids."

She returned it to the shelf and fluffed her hair, wishing for a brush. She reached into her purse and pulled out her compact mirror and lip gloss. Not until she was presentable did she answer him. "How unexpected! Where are you?"

"I'm in the children's section. It's story time."

"Care for adult company?" Marc responded with a smiley face. "Come on over. I'm saving a seat for you."

She straightened her pencil skirt and silk blouse, grateful she chose to dress up a bit today. Most Sundays, she spent in yoga pants and oversized t-shirts.

Brushing one more wrinkle from her skirt, she tiptoed around the corner and entered the children's corner of the store. A large tree was painted on the bright blue wall and adorned with squirrels, birds, and playful deer. About fifty children sat on the bright green carpet in front of a gray-haired lady reading a book by Dr. Seuss. She spoke in a soft but strong teacher's voice and made grand gestures to animate the story as she turned the pages. The children and the adults all sat wide-mouthed.

Traci's phone beeped, and she realized she had been staring.

Another text from Marc. "I'm sitting two rows in front of you."

With a rush of heat to her face, she noticed him, turned around in his chair, waving her over.

She slipped into the seat next to him. "Hey."

"Hey there."

Her heart bounced in her chest when he leaned over and kissed her left cheek.

"Am I embarrassing you?"

She suppressed a giggle. He held her hand.

Warmth spread throughout her body. His touch calmed her nerves.

They sat next to each other and listened to the children's book. Fifteen minutes later, the story hour was over. The reader dismissed the children, who jumped to their feet like hot tamales and rushed to either the surrounding bookshelf, play area, or their parents.

Two of the most adorable kids, one sweet-faced boy and one joyful girl, rushed to Marc. They spoke in unison with equaled enthusiasm. "Uncle Marky!"

Marc released his grasp on Traci and scooped the kids into his lap, the boy on one knee, the girl on the other.

The girl bounced, her curls keeping time. "Did you like the story?"

Marc chuckled. "Did you like it?"

"Yes." She twitched her nose, so much like Marc's angular one.

The boy spoke in a high voice. "I liked the story too."

"Good."

The girl stared at Traci. "Who are you?"

"My name is Traci."

The girl reached out for Traci, who looked to Marc for approval. Once he gave it, she accepted the child onto her lap.

"My name is Samantha."

"Nice to meet you."

Samantha pointed at the young boy who nestled against Marc's chest. "And that's my little brother Regan. He's a big baby." She tapped Marc's shoulder. "I like her, Uncle Marky. She smells like strawberries."

The color in Marc's cheeks heightened. "I like her too."

Traci's stomach performed somersaults.

"Do you like my Uncle Marky?"

"Yes, I do."

Regan snored. Marc shrugged. "Time for me to get these two home for a nap."

Samantha stuck out her lower lip. "But I want to stay here and look at books with Traci."

"We'll have to do that another time." Marc stood. "It's time to go."

Samantha harrumphed. "Can we play some time?"

How did she answer that question? He hadn't called. Did he want to spend more time with her? She glanced at him. He nodded. A little tingle raced through her arms. "That sounds great."

A bright smile spread across Samantha's face. "Good." She hugged Traci, jumped off her lap, and clutched her uncle's hand, waving goodbye.

"I'll call you. I really will. There was a family emergency. My sister was in a car accident and is in the hospital."

"Oh, no. I hope her injuries aren't too serious."

"She broke her leg and had surgery. In a few days, she'll be home. I hope you understand."

"Of course." Here she worried about whether or not he liked her, when he was taking care of his sister and her kids. "Family comes first."

His shoulders relaxed. "Thanks for understanding. We'll talk soon."

"I'm looking forward to your call."

They sauntered out of the children's area, Regan asleep on Marc's shoulder, Samantha tagging along. Like a family. A family she could get used to being a part of.

"Who was that?"

She jumped. Carla's voice tore Traci out of her thoughts.

"Sorry, sweetie. Didn't mean to scare you." Carla sat beside her in the empty story time area.

She played with her purse strap. "That was Marc. And his sister Gina's kids."

Carla sucked in her breath. "That handsome fella was your Marc?"

"Yes. Dreamy, I know."

"Whew." Carla fanned herself. "I think I need fresh air."

"Stop being so dramatic."

"You've got to tell him. Do it sooner rather than later. You don't want to lose him. He's a natural with those kids. I can totally see you two happily married and having a bunch of your own."

Her stomach started with some weird somersaults. "The thing is, so can I. But I can't tell him yet."

"Are you praying about this?"

Traci shook her head.

"You better start praying about it today."

Traci focused on the circle-patterned carpet.

"What's wrong?"

"My relationship with God is not the best lately."

"What do you mean?"

Traci toed the rug. "I haven't prayed as often since Greg left me."

"Why not?"

"I thought Greg was the one for me. Then he stood me up at the altar and ran off with my best friend. I feel like an idiot. I prayed about our relationship and thanked God for sending him into my life. It just feels like—"

"Stop."

Traci stilled.

"Forget about Greg. If anything, God protected you from a deeper hurt and divorce. Look at you now. Five months later, he sends you Marc. And from what I saw by observing him today, he's a man of integrity who's good with kids. Greg is nothing like Marc, and Marc is definitely nothing like Greg. If you ask me, Marc is the answer to the prayers you never prayed. God's answering the desires of your heart, sweetie."

"That makes sense. A lot of sense."

Too much sense. Carla was probably right. She needed to tell Marc. Soon.

~

Marc pulled the covers over Regan and kissed his head. To his surprise, the kids got ready for bed without a fuss, even after their nap this afternoon. Samantha was already fast asleep.

He slipped out of his nephew's room, went downstairs to the living room, plopped onto the couch, and kicked off his shoes.

He grabbed his cell phone from the coffee table, remembering his interaction with Traci at the bookstore earlier that day. Just what he needed.

The kids loved her too. Amazing. None of his ex-girlfriends were good with children. Most of them never talked about having some of their own. Samantha took right to her, as if she were long lost family.

He finger-combed his hair. He'd never fallen for a girl this fast. He needed to slow down. The last thing he wanted to do was get too serious too soon and then lose her because of it.

Scrolling through their conversation, he remembered he never answered her question when she first texted him in the bookstore. She asked for his sister's last name. He typed in the answer. "Braxton."

Seconds later, Traci replied. "What?"

"My sister Gina's last name is Braxton. Didn't you say that you were looking for her books earlier today but didn't know her last name?"

Traci sent a blushing smiley face. "Yes, that's right. Thank you!"

"You're welcome. When can I see you?"

Traci answered with a winking emoticon. "You just saw me today."

"I know. It was wonderful. When can I see you again?"

"That depends."

"On what?

"If you remember to call me."

"I'm talking to you now."

"Real men don't text."

Marc laughed. "I'll call you tomorrow."

"Sounds like a plan. Hey, Marc?"

"Yes?"

"I need to tell you something."

"Go ahead. I'm all ears."

A few minutes passed without a text from her.

"Traci?"

"Never mind. It's not important to tell you right now."

His stomach clenched in that old, familiar way. "Is everything okay?"

"No. I mean yes. I mean, don't worry about me. We can talk later. Goodnight."

"Okay. Goodnight." Marc laid his phone to rest.

What did she have to tell him?

Probably the words he'd heard far too many times.

Chapter 8

Traci pulled her coat tighter and buttoned it after stepping out of her car. She crossed the parking lot outside of the department store in short order. Once inside, warmth of the store's heating met her, and she let out a sigh of relief. She fluffed her hair before strolling over to the jewelry department.

She was looking for a new necklace. But she paused when she reached the engagement ring display. Memories rushed back. Greg took her to a store in Annapolis just two years ago. He used his business connections to shut the place down to retail customers and have one full hour reserved for him to pull off the most romantic proposal she ever saw.

She rubbed her finger as memories of him placing the rose carat ring on her hand flooded in. If she had married Greg... She wiped away a tear that escaped her eye and forced herself to refocus on her present reality. Greg left her at the altar on their wedding day and ran off with her former best friend. She was better off without him.

She strolled to the other side of the counter, toward the necklaces. As she turned the corner, she bumped into a familiar-looking man. Same sharp-cut brown hair. Same athletic build.

Marc turned around. "We've got to stop doing this."

She couldn't keep the smile from her voice. "We must keep running into each other for a reason. Why are you here today?"

"We're looking for a gift for Gina."

"We?" Traci looked around. She only saw him.

"Yeah, I brought the kids. They're just a few steps away, looking at the watches."

As if on cue, Samantha's voice rang out. "Uncle Marky. We found the best watch for Mommy."

"She sure is enthusiastic." Then again, with him for an uncle, who wouldn't be?

"It's not a problem, is it?" Darkness swept through his eyes.

"Just the opposite."

He brightened. "Come on, then." He grasped her by the hand.

She loved his strong yet gentle clasp. Together, they meandered a few steps around the corner to the watch display. Samantha's eyes twinkled when she saw Traci. She dropped the case containing the wristwatch on the floor and rushed to her. "It's you!"

Samantha hugged her around her waist so hard that Traci teetered, almost losing her balance. Regan looked on with his thumb in his mouth. Marc reached down to pick up the case from the floor.

"Yes, it's me. How are you, Samantha?"

"We missed you. Uncle Marky missed you too."

Marc's face blazed red. He busied himself with peering at the watches in the glass case.

Traci pulled herself from Samantha's embrace and knelt down to be at eye level. "Hey, I promised that we'd meet again, remember?"

A bright smile spread across the little girl's fair face. "Yes, I remember. You said you would play with me. But today, we're here to buy a gift for Mommy. She's coming home from the hospital tonight."

"That's wonderful news. I'm glad to hear that she's doing better."

"Yeah, me too. Me and Regan missed our Mommy."

Traci rubbed Samantha's upper back. "I'm sure you did."

Samantha grabbed Traci and led her a few feet to where Marc stood with Regan holding onto his pant legs, his thumb in his mouth. Marc handed Samantha the case, which she presented to Traci, her blue eyes shining. "This is what we're going to buy Mommy. Do you like it?"

Traci examined the silver watch with a band design of red hearts. "It's lovely. I like it very much."

Samantha beamed. She cradled the case in her hands and turned to Marc. "Uncle Marky, you should buy Traci a ring."

Traci couldn't breathe. His Adam's apple worked up and down. A long moment passed before the color in his face returned to normal. "Let's buy this watch for your Mommy first."

He flashed Traci a crooked smile and mouthed the words, "I'm sorry."

She shook her head and mouthed back, "It's okay."

Marc and his little charges waved goodbye and moved to the cash register.

She let out a low breath. Samantha had no idea what she just said, but it reminded Traci of her secret. A secret she had to tell Marc before things got serious between them, just in case one day in the future he would like to buy her a ring.

She wrangled her phone from the depths of her purse and texted Carla while she walked farther into the store toward the shoe department. "You'll never guess who I just ran into at Macy's."

"Marc."

Traci peered around in case Carla lurked behind the blouse rack. "How did you know?"

"Lucky guess. What's up?"

"He was shopping with the kids for a gift for their mom."

"That's right. He was with kids at the bookstore. Is he married?"

"No, silly. He's single. His sister is a widow. He babysits her kids."

"Wow, you found yourself a real Renaissance man, didn't you?"

"Yeah. Looks like it."

Traci wandered through the crowded shoe department, intent on her conversation with Carla. She sidestepped a bunch of boxes strewn across her path.

Well, she sidestepped almost all of them. One

tripped her up. She stumbled, dropped the phone, and braced herself for a bad fall. Instead, she landed in strong and lean arms.

A familiar voice spoke, tickling her memory. "Careful there, miss."

Her blood turned icy. She struggled to pull herself out of his embrace without turning around. But it was too late. He was already peering around to see her. "Traci?"

She stood tall and steeled herself, greeting him in a voice that she hoped was steady and emotionless. "Greg."

"Traci, I—"

"Traci!" A little girl's exclamation cut off Greg.

And there came Samantha, running toward her, Marc right behind, holding a sleeping Regan in his arms.

This had to be a movie. A really bad movie where the ex-fiancé stands face-to-face with the jilted bride's new love interest and the star of the movie is caught in the middle.

Samantha rushed to Traci and gave her a big hug. "We wanted to say goodbye."

Traci managed what she hoped was a pleasant smile. She reached down and wiped a strand of Samantha's wispy honey-brown hair out of her eyes. "Goodbye, sweet face."

She turned to Marc. "She called me sweet face." She looked back at Traci. "What does that mean?"

Traci tried to stop her hands from shaking.

Greg cleared his throat. He wanted an introduction.

"Marc, this is Greg. Greg, this is Marc."

A few seconds of silence followed as the men sized each other up, examining each other like lions. Circling. Analyzing the competition. Claiming their territory.

Greg gestured to shake Marc's hand. "I'm her ex-fiancé. Who are you?"

Marc tugged on his ear. "I'm her friend."

That iciness in her mid-section intensified. Friend? She thought they were more than friends.

Greg smirked, then winked. Her stomach knotted.

"Nice seeing you, darling. Until next time." Greg sauntered away.

She clenched her fists. How dare he act that way toward her, so cavalier, so all-knowing, so . . .

The room spun. She reached for the rack. Marc put Regan down and moved toward her. "Traci, are you okay?"

The blackness consumed her.

~

Traci opened her eyes. Where was she? What happened? A cool breeze caressed her face. She sat up. She and Marc rested on a bench a few yards away from the gated perimeter of the mall's outdoor playground. Samantha and Regan swung on the monkey bars, laughing.

Traci squeezed her pounding head. Marc handed her a cup of orange juice.

"What happened?" She sipped the juice.

"You fainted. I carried you out here to get some fresh air."

"I'm sorry. Time got away from me this morning, and I didn't have breakfast. I just remember Greg. Then, nothing."

Marc rubbed the top of her hand. "What's going on?"

I could ask you the same question, friend. "My ex, Greg. He . . ."

Marc straightened and leaned in. "Did he hurt you? Because I will find him and hurt him."

Wait a minute. This was not the type of reaction a person who is just a friend would have in the situation. "Why? We're just friends, remember?"

Marc's eyes lost their shimmer. "I'm sorry. I don't know why I said that." He brushed a few stray strands of her hair away from her face. "I care about you more than a friend. I would like for you to be my girlfriend. You know, go steady? If the kids even still say that these days."

Her heart thumped in an erratic pattern. "Really?"

"Yes. If it's what you want."

"I'd like that."

"Me too."

"About Greg."

"I don't need to know."

"If we're going to be open and honest with each other, then you do need to know."

Inside, she grimaced at the weight of her words. She could tell him about Greg now, but she could not share her secret. Not after the drama in the store. If Marc knew about her inheritance at this point, he'd grab his sister's kids and leave, never to be seen again. She bit her bottom lip. Right now, she would at least tell him about Greg.

"A few months ago, I was engaged to Greg. I

thought he . . . I thought he was the one God wanted me to marry. Everything was perfect until . . ."

She sucked in a deep breath and stared at her hands, which shook. "Until he left me at the altar on our wedding day and ran off with my maid of honor."

Marc clenched his fists. He stood up and kicked the dust. He then turned to Traci. "Where is he?"

"He's long gone, Marc. It doesn't matter anymore. We're through."

Marc's eyes blazed. "If I ever see him again, I will pummel him."

Could it be that he cared? That he wanted to watch over her and protect her? That he wouldn't hurt her?

He relaxed his shoulders. "I'm sorry." He closed the distance between them and touched her face, his caress light and soft. "I just don't want to see you hurt."

The chatter and shouts of the children on the playground faded as he closed in and kissed her, his lips grazing hers. He deepened the kiss. Her heart fluttered so fast she thought she'd faint again.

He pulled away and looked at her as if she was the only woman in the world.

All she wanted to say stuck in her throat.

"Uncle Marky!"

Marc let out a low chuckle as Samantha and Regan called from the playground. "Can we go home now?"

Marc jogged over to the kids and helped them climb down from the monkey bars. Traci couldn't breathe. The blood whooshed in her ears, the sound

so loud she couldn't hear herself think.
But the unsaid words echoed in her heart.
He loves me.

Chapter 9

Upbeat music played throughout the popular gym that Marc frequented. Men grunted as they lifted weights, and women chatted with each other as they worked out on the treadmill and elliptical machines. The smell of stale socks and sweaty bodies hung in the air.

Toward the far corner of the large gym, Marc lay on his back, bench-pressing the heavy weights. Victor stood behind him, leaning over the bar to spot him as he worked out.

"Forty-nine," Marc counted between breaths. "Fifty!"

Victor grasped the bar and helped Marc return it to the rack. Marc breathed a deep sigh of relief.

His friend shook his head. "Don't breathe too easy. You've got five more reps."

Marc groaned and reached for the cool steel bar again. "Why do I put myself through this torture?" His triceps tensed as he put all his effort into lifting the weights.

"Because you want to be in prime shape for your lovely lady. How is she, by the way?"

"You mean Traci?"

"Who else?"

Marc gritted his teeth as he hoisted the weights into the air. "She's great."

"So, when's the wedding?"

"Wedding?"

"Yeah, I have a good feeling about this one."

Marc continued bench pressing. He paused to take a breath before answering.

"I don't know."

Victor's eyes widened. "What's to know? She's perfect for you."

Marc rested the bar on the rack and leaned forward. "All of my girlfriends broke up with me, claiming to just want to be friends. What if Traci does the same?"

Victor moved around the bench to stand in front of him. "Traci is nothing like your exes. She's the real deal, man."

Marc wiped the sweat beads on his forehead with his soft, spring-smelling towel. "She is pretty wonderful."

Victor snapped his towel at Marc. "Then what are you waiting for, man? Propose to her before some other guy moves in."

Marc rubbed the back of his sore neck. "It's too soon."

"Hey, when you know, you know."

Victor returned to his place behind Marc to spot him. He leaned over before Marc lifted the weights. "At least she's not a gold-digger."

Marc just about dropped the weight. Victor scrambled to help him steady it. Marc gulped. "What did you say?"

"I said, at least she's not a gold-digger. You know, not after your money." Victor helped Marc rest the weight on the rack.

Marc snorted. "I'm an entry-level journalist still paying my dues. I have no money."

"I hear you, man."

Marc reached for the weights and resumed his work-out. Though Victor meant them as a joke, a little thought ruminated in the back of his mind. What if Traci were a gold-digger? They were both entry level journalists, so it wasn't like either of them had money. But what if?

No, she wouldn't use him for money. He had none. He pushed the crazy idea aside. No more thinking about this. She'd proven herself to him. And he loved her.

The weight wobbled as Marc's thoughts voiced what was in his heart. He loved her.

Victor steadied the barbell. "What's wrong, man?"

Wrong? He loved her. But what if she broke up with him?

Marc returned the weight to the rack and sat up. "I think I've had enough for today."

"But you've got one more set."

Marc took off in the direction of the locker room. "I need a break."

And time to himself to pray. He needed God to show him if Traci was the one for him.

~

Traci stared at the inheritance letter on her kitchen table. She'd shoved it into her desk drawer the day her mother had given it to her and tried to forget about it.

Until now.

If only it didn't have that stipulation. The one about being married.

Memories of their time together and their first kiss replayed in her mind's movie theater. He loved her. She had to trust that he knew she loved him too.

It was time to tell Marc about the letter.

Deep down, all the way to her big toe, she knew it was.

She loved him too much to keep this a secret from him any longer.

But how? Even as a professional writer, she couldn't think of the right words to say or how to even begin to broach this topic. Her gaze moved from the letter to her cell phone.

There was one person who would know. She dialed the number.

Carla answered with a yawn, redefining groggy. "Hello?"

"Hey. Did I wake you?" She glanced at the clock and grimaced. Ten o'clock.

Another yawn. "Yeah, you did."

Traci fingered the edge of the letter. "I'm sorry. We can talk tomorrow."

"No, girl. You already woke me up. Speak now."

"I appreciate your sense of humor and availability to talk." She drew a deep breath. "I know I need to tell Marc about my inheritance letter."

"Um, yeah."

"I just don't know how." She got up and circled the table.

"Here's how. You tell him. Get it out of your system. Tell him the truth and nothing but the truth. Just let it out."

Traci's hands trembled. "But what if he gets mad at me and leaves me?"

"Why would he get mad at you?"

"Sheesh, Carla. You know this would upset anyone."

"Not a man who loves you. Who wants to spend the rest of his life with you."

"Marc does love me."

"My point exactly. So tell him already, and go live happily ever after."

The phone slid in Traci's grasp. Her damp hands couldn't hold it anymore. She switched to speakerphone. "I can't. I want to, but I can't, because I cannot stand the thought of losing him."

A big, prolonged sigh sounded from Carla. "Get yourself together, girl. The man loves you. If it's the kind of love that will last a lifetime, he'll understand."

Maybe she was overthinking Marc's reaction. He may not be bothered by this news at all. In fact, he may even like it.

"Hello? Traci?"

"I'm still here."

"Well?"

"Well, I think you'd better go back to bed."

"And?"

A small smile tugged at the corner of Traci's lips. Imagine all the positive possibilities that could come out of her revealing the truth. They could build a wonderful life together. Maybe Carla was right.

"And?"

Carla's voice jolted Traci out her private thoughts. "And I think I better tell Marc the truth."

"Yes, girl. Do it tomorrow."

"Tomorrow?"

"Yes, tomorrow, before you chicken out."

Traci laughed. "Good night, Carla."

"Good night. I'll pray for you too."

"Thanks for being such a good friend." What would she do without her?

"Mm, hm. I'd make a good bridesmaid too."

"I'm sure you would."

They said their goodbyes, and the dial tone sounded. Traci pressed the end button on her phone.

She took her inheritance letter, folded it, and returned it to its place in the manila envelope.

Lord, let this be the right move.

Chapter 10

Traci sat at her desk in the office, sipping her chai latte and staring at her computer screen, working on a story that was due before quitting time. She took another long sip of the sweet drink. The cursor on the empty page had blinked at her for five minutes. Any longer and someone might say something about her lack of productivity.

How could she concentrate on work when all she could think of was how Marc would react when she told him her secret tonight.

"Traci?"

She jumped. Her cup teetered on the edge of the desk. Just before it spilled all over her keyboard, she steadied it and placed it on her desk. "Carla? Now that you've put me into cardiac arrest, what do you want?"

"Sorry. I didn't mean to startle you."

"It's okay. What's up?"

Carla leaned against the left side of Traci's cubicle. She spoke in a hushed tone. "Did you hear?"

Traci frowned. "Hear about what?"

"Calvin is laying people off. Our colleagues have been buzzing about this news all morning."

Traci sat up straight. "What?"

Carla shrugged. "We work at a newspaper in the digital age. Times are tough. I heard that it's problems with the budget. The CEO cannot afford to write all of our checks any longer. So, she's ordering Calvin to let people go."

"How many?"

"I heard that it's all of the newest hired and then a few underperformers."

Sweat formed on Traci's forehead. "Newest hired?" The words squeaked out. She'd been working here for five years. But the *Maryland Times* hadn't hired anyone else in about five years. So did that mean…?

Oh, no.

Carla reached out and touched Traci's shoulder. "Don't worry. You're an excellent reporter. Surely Calvin will keep you."

Easy for her to say. She'd been here for a decade, and she was a star reporter. She didn't have to worry about Calvin firing her.

Traci turned to face her computer. She refused to let her imagination run wild. "Thanks for the info, Carla. I need to finish a story now."

Carla nodded. "Okay."

Traci listened to Carla's footfalls until she couldn't hear her anymore. Then, she closed her eyes and rubbed her temples. She could not afford to be laid off. She could barely pay her bills.

And she refused to let her parents help. They'd worked hard toward retirement. She wouldn't take that money from them.

The ringing of the phone interrupted her thoughts. Calvin Rivers' name popped up on the caller ID.

Her body went cold. "Good morning, Calvin."

"Good morning, Traci. Please see me in my office."

"Yes, sir."

She said a silent prayer, then rose to her feet. She zig-zagged through the maze of cubicles toward Calvin's corner office. Was it just her imagination, or were her fellow reporters looking at her with sympathy in their eyes? Did they know something that she didn't?

Avoiding their gazes, she held her head high and strode into Calvin's office.

He gazed at her from his seat behind his mahogany desk. "Close the door behind you."

She obliged.

"Have a seat."

She slumped into the chair in front of his desk.

Calvin took off his reading glasses, folded his hands on top of his desk, and made eye contact with Traci.

Her hands trembled under his stare. She clasped them together in her lap.

"There's no easy way to say this. You're being laid off."

Traci's world crashed like a tidal wave on the shore. Her heart rate accelerated. "Why?"

Calvin leaned back in his chair and sighed. "Our

CEO is making some changes to better suit her budget. I have no choice but to let the newest hires go."

"But, but I've been here for five years."

"Yes, I know, and you've done an excellent job. But there's really no way that I can keep you under the CEO's new budget."

"I'll take a pay cut."

Calvin shook his head. "That wouldn't help."

She stared at her quaking hands, willing the waterworks away. "But I need this job." Her voice was little more than a whisper.

Calvin leaned forward.

"I'm sorry. We have to let you go."

She nodded her head.

"You have two weeks remaining and one final paycheck before you need to pack your belongings and leave."

She nodded again. She could do nothing else.

"That will be all."

Another nod. She rose, turned around, and exited Calvin's office. As she hurried through the maze of cubicles, she ignored the stares from her colleagues. She sped past her desk and made a beeline for the women's bathroom.

Once there, she locked herself inside a stall and wept.

~

Marc climbed the stairs to Traci's fourth floor apartment, balancing the two, big, brown grocery-sized bags of takeout food from Traci's favorite Indian restaurant. He'd offered to take her out to dinner, but when he spoke to her, she said that she'd rather stay home.

So, he decided to surprise her with her favorite meal. Basmati rice, chapatti, and lamb chops. Good food always made her feel better. He approached her door and knocked at it with his foot since his hands weren't free.

"Who is it?"

"The man of your dreams." Marc chuckled.

"Not now, Marc. I just want to be left alone."

Did something happen? What was wrong with her?

"Open the door, Trace. I've brought something that will cheer you up." He paused, but only got silence in return. "It's your favorite dish from that Indian restaurant. It's still hot."

The locks ground, and Traci opened the door. She didn't look him in his face, but stepped aside and let him enter.

She wasn't fine. At all. "What's wrong?"

She closed the door but never even as much as glanced at him.

"I'm going to put these bags down and get dinner ready. Why don't you sit down and talk to me?" He followed through with what he said.

Traci slunk into a seat at her kitchen table and covered her face. With shuddered sobs, she cried.

He left the bags and went to her side. He took her in his arms and stroked her hair. "What's wrong, sweetheart?"

She hiccupped out the words. "I…lost…my…job."

He pulled back. "I'm so sorry. What happened?"

She stared at his shirt and inhaled a deep breath,

controlling her crying. "The newspaper is going through a round of layoffs. The newest hired are the first to go."

Her words struck at his heart. It was hard to be a newspaper journalist, but how could a good reporter be laid off? He never realized she was a recent hire. "I'm sorry, honey."

For the first time that night, she met his gaze. Her beautiful hazel eyes swam with tears. "I don't know how I'm going to pay my bills or my rent. I still have those wedding debts to settle. Greg isn't contributing a thing. What am I going to do?"

She nestled into his shoulder. He held her close and kissed her forehead. "I'll take care of you."

Her soft tears soaked his shirt. "I can't ask you to do that. You're an entry-level journalist yourself. I know your salary isn't enough to support anyone other than you." She pulled back. "Besides, it's not like you're obligated to support me. We're not married."

A fresh round of sobs tore from her. She ran down the hall, her door slamming shut.

He scrubbed his face. What could he do to help her? He didn't know where to begin. Maybe she needed some time to herself. Maybe if he unpacked the food and put it away, he'd think of something.

He turned toward the kitchen. A manila envelope on the floor near the table caught his eye. He reached down and picked it up. Two sheets of paper slipped out and fluttered to the floor.

He picked the papers up, meaning to place them in the envelope. The return address caught his eye. Chadwick Law Offices. What was this? Why would she need a lawyer?

Was she in trouble?

Just a peek at the papers, just to know if she needed his help.

The words on the page struck him, robbing him of his breath.

An inheritance letter.

And Traci needed to be married before she could receive the money? What did that mean?

Victor's words rang in his head. *At least she's not a gold digger.* Marc went cold, then hot.

How could she do this to him? She loved him. At least, that's what she'd led him to believe. But it looked like she was just using him.

He couldn't believe it.

Victor's words had become reality.

Traci was nothing more than a gold digger.

And now that she'd lost her job, she'd be hustling him to the altar in double time.

Traci re-entered the kitchen with a tissue box in her hands and a wavering smile on her face. "Thanks for being here for me. I just needed a minute alone. I'm ready to eat if you are."

He clenched the letter.

"Marc?"

She stepped to the kitchen table. "What's wrong?"

He held the paper out to her. "What's this?"

"Are you snooping?" Her eyes darkened.

"Are you keeping secrets?"

She sunk into the chair across from him, tracing the stain from a wet glass. "I'm sorry. I was going to tell you about my inheritance letter. I really was, but it never seemed like the right time." He placed the letter on the table on top of the manila envelope. "Now is as good a time as ever."

She nodded and drew in a deep breath. "My mom gave me the letter a few months ago, before I met you. When I met you and we started seeing each other, I...I fell in love with you, and I didn't want to hurt you."

He bit his lip.

"So I kept it a secret from you because I know that you value honesty and—"

"So you lied to me? You just wanted to get me to propose to you so you could be rich?"

"No, that's not what I meant."

Marc sat back and folded his arms. "Well then, what did you mean?"

"I was going to tell you. Tonight in fact, and then I lost my job and—"

"So you had the letter out, knowing marrying me would solve all of your problems."

"No, I had it out so I could tell you about it."

"I don't know what is the truth and what is a lie anymore. I need to go."

She reached out to him, but he stepped away.

"Marc, please don't leave."

He pushed past her, right out the door, banging it shut behind him. His dream girl hadn't been honest with him. Despite what she said, he couldn't shake the thoughts that she was using him.

He rushed down the four flights of stairs and burst through the building's exit. The chilly breeze of the autumn night met him, cooling his hot face.

Above him, the stars twinkled in the night sky.

Why, God? Why this? Why now?

Chapter 11

Traci stared at her second to last paycheck and rubbed the back of her neck. It wasn't much. But she was just one paycheck away from making zero dollars until she could find a new job. She bit her bottom lip.

If only her grandfather hadn't put in that stipulation for the inheritance. It would solve all of her financial problems and make her dreams come true. Dreams like owning her own bookstore like she promised Hallee.

Hallee, her cousin who was like the sister she never had. Traci swallowed around the lump in her throat as she thought of their last conversation before Hallee's cancer returned with a vengeance.

The girls had giggled as they shared their secrets in their makeshift tent in Hallee's home library. They poured over their latest favorite books underneath the blankets they propped over chairs as their tent. They each held a flashlight over their books and discussed the characters.

Suddenly, Hallee shut her book. She looked at Traci with a serious stare that stole her breath. "What?"

"When I die, please remember our dream for our bookstore and make it come true when you grow up."

Traci clutched her book. "Oh Hallee, you're not going to die. You're going to beat this cancer and grow up with me. Then we'll open the bookstore together, just like we planned."

Hallee's eyes remained dark and serious. "Promise me."

Traci shook her head.

"Promise me."

With everything in her, Traci didn't want to make the vow. But the single tear trickling down her cousin's face swayed her. "I promise."

Hallee's grin had been almost as bright as the sun. "And you can call it Hallee's House. Named after me."

"I will."

"Long day?"

Traci jerked, and she straightened. Carla's question shocked her back into reality. "Ever try knocking?"

"There's no door. You're in a cubicle."

"Oh, right."

"What's going on? I see you got your paycheck. Is that why you're depressed?"

"I'm not depressed." She shoved the envelope into her purse. "I'm just disappointed. I barely make enough money to support myself. Our career's system of paying your dues is hurting me. Not that it matters. I'm only two weeks away from being unemployed."

Carla reached over and gave Traci a hug.

"I hear you, girl. But what else is hurting you?"

Traci furrowed her brows.

Carla returned to her favorite spot, leaning against the cubicle wall.

"I have no idea what you're asking."

"Spill it."

Traci glanced over the other cubicles. Too many prying ears. "Follow me to the break room."

They entered, the aroma of coffee, usually enticing, now churning her stomach. Traci shut the door and paced.

"I'm waiting."

She stopped in her tracks. "I finally told Marc about my secret."

"Really? When?"

"One week ago."

"How did it go?"

Traci rubbed the conference tabletop. "Not so good."

Carla touched her upper arm. "What happened?"

"He left. He didn't talk to me for days." She pinched the bridge of her nose.

"Is he talking to you now?"

Traci wiped away the tears that eked out. "He called me last weekend, but hung up before I could answer. I've called and called, but he won't answer. He broke my . . . heart. Just like . . . Greg."

Carla pulled Traci close for a comforting hug. "Oh honey, Marc is nothing like Greg."

"I know." She swiped at her tears. "But he still

left me, and it was like being jilted all over again."

"But Marc was probably just upset. He needed time to process what you told him, so he took a break. But he did call you."

"He hung up."

"He must still love you. He'll call again. Don't compare him to that lowlife ex-fiancé of yours. From what I see, your Marc is a true gentleman."

Traci sucked in air to stop from hyperventilating. She pulled away from Carla, stared at the ceiling, dried her eyes. "Really? You think so?"

"I think he loves you more than your secret."

"I guess you're right. But it hurts so much. I love him, and he wounded me when he walked out on me."

Carla rubbed Traci's arm. "Remember, your secret blindsided him too. He's had a lot to deal with and to sift through. But I believe you can work through this. Love conquers all."

Traci managed a timid smile. "Love conquers all?"

"Always."

~

Marc lounged in the small, simple break room at work, munching on his rather soggy cheese sandwich. Out in the office, telephones rang, people chatted in low voices, and keyboards clacked. But today, he was numb. Even the aroma of fresh-brewed Brazilian coffee didn't perk him up.

He glanced at his phone, checked his messages. Five of them. Two texts, three voicemails. All from Traci.

He bit the inside of his cheek, tasting blood.

Victor entered the room. "Woman problems?" He scraped back the plastic chair beside Marc and sat.

"Why would you say that?"

"You've been depressed for two weeks straight."

Marc opened his bag of potato chips, the salt stinging a paper cut on his thumb. "It's her."

"You mean Traci?"

"Yep."

"What happened?"

"I'm not at liberty to say. All I can tell you is that we broke up. Or I think we did."

"Why?"

"She lied to me. I walked out, and we haven't spoken since."

"I can't blame you."

"I called her once. Why, I don't know. I hung up before she answered. Now, she keeps calling me. But I'm not ready to talk."

"Well, then. Not much I can tell you there, buddy. But if you love this girl, don't wait too long to call her. At least find out what she wants. Maybe she's ready to beg for your forgiveness."

"I'm not holding my breath." Marc slurped his water.

Victor pulled the top off his coffee and stirred in a packet of sugar. "Did you hear about the advancement opportunity?"

"No. What's going on?"

"Anne is looking to promote her hardest working journalist to a chief correspondent position in the politics section of the *Chicago Reporter*."

Marc almost spit out his drink. He covered

politics now. So he had the experience. His family lived in Chicago, where he grew up. If he got the promotion, it would be like returning home.

And now would be the perfect time to get out of town.

Victor leaned in. "I think you should go for it. Let Anne know you're interested."

What a great opportunity. Maybe God's way of saying he needed to move on from Traci. Start fresh. "I will."

Chapter 12

Traci parked her car in the lot surrounding the hotel in downtown Bowie. She sighed. Congressman Wright and his entourage should arrive any minute now to honor fifteen educators, both teachers and principals, who received the *Maryland Times'* Teacher of the Year Award.

This was to be her last assignment.

A sign greeted her in the lobby with directions to the conference room. She moved down the hall, present in body but on autopilot as she had been for the past seven days. Marc didn't return her seven calls or ten text messages. Maybe she shouldn't have told him about the inheritance. She risked everything and lost it all.

She hoped he would forgive her, but it looked like forgiveness was not his strong suit. And apparently, neither was communication after he'd been hurt.

She clung to her purse strap and willed herself not to cry. She was on assignment for the newspaper. She could not afford to let her emotions get the best of her. Not here and not now.

She inhaled and exhaled several times before arriving at the designated room. Two of the congressman's staff members sat at a table just outside of the heavy double doors.

"Good morning. I'm Traci Hightower, a reporter for the *Maryland Times*. Where do I sign in?"

The shorter lady handed a pen to Traci and pointed to the paper on a clipboard. The taller woman handed Traci a press kit.

"Thank you."

She held the folder close to her chest as she entered the room. Four long tables formed a large rectangle with a big gap in the middle. Nametags sat on the table in front of each chair. Traci found her place and slipped into the chair behind it.

She unloaded the essential items from her purse: the digital voice recorder, her reporter's notepad, and a blue ink pen. But as she reached for her bottle of water, a very familiar member of the media walked in.

Her mouth went dry.

Marc.

God, help me.

She focused on her pad of paper, pretending to take notes. *Lord, give me the strength to not crumble on the outside.*

Inside, her stomach tossed and turned.

He moved in her direction. She glanced at the nametag on the table beside hers.

Marc Roberts.

Sheesh.

"Traci."

She pursed her lips.

He took the seat next to her.

Still, she avoided his gaze. "Marc." Her voice squeaked.

Congressman Wright entered the room and strolled over to his place. Good. The ceremony was about to start. All she had to do was focus on what was in front of her and forget about the colleague who sat to her left side, close to her heart.

The one who refused to talk to her.

Congressman Wright greeted everyone before starting his speech. "Maryland's public schools are rated as the best in the nation for five years in a row now. Our dedicated teachers and principals who go above and beyond the call of duty are to thank for this great accomplishment. Today, I am pleased to recognize these extraordinary educators. We are here to discuss what we can do to continue strengthening our school system and ensuring that all students can succeed."

Traci jotted notes as the congressman spoke. She dropped her pen and bent to pick it up, glancing at Marc. Who stared at her.

In a flash, he turned away and scribbled in his notepad.

So, he could stare at her but not talk to her? The nerve of the man.

In a sheer act of willpower, she zoned into her work and tuned out her heart's emotions for Marc. Before she knew it, the press conference and ceremony were over.

She made her way around the room with the

digital voice recorder, interviewing the top five people whom she thought would contribute the most to her story.

Forty minutes later, she wrapped up her last interview with a hearty handshake. She relaxed her shoulders. These were the days she loved her job. Great quotes, interactions with distinguished people, learning more from their stories. She would miss this. As she gathered her papers and things, she glanced up.

Only she and Marc remained in the conference room.

Great.

With as much speed as possible, she grabbed her purse and reporter gear. She turned to leave. He reached out and touched her arm.

She froze. Her heartbeat accelerated. What did he want? She could not face him here, not now, especially when his touch charged her emotions.

"Traci, I—"

If he wouldn't talk to her, she wouldn't speak to him. "Goodbye, Marc." Without a backward glance, she strode from the room and quickened her pace until she reached her car. She opened the door and slid in behind the steering wheel. She placed her purse and press kit in the passenger's seat and allowed herself to do what she refused to inside the hotel.

She cried.

~

Marc stood alone on the far end of the hotel's parking lot. He kicked the dust.

He didn't expect to see Traci today covering the

same story. And he definitely didn't expect for his emotions to take the rollercoaster ride that seeing her started.

He gazed heavenward.

Why God? Why now? After all the trials with dishonesty that I experienced with my ex-girlfriends, you bring me this woman, and I fall for her. Hard. But then I find out that she's keeping secrets too. Why does this keep happening to me?

Because he cared.

He steadied himself against his car. He wouldn't be so upset right now if he didn't harbor feelings for Traci. And love her he did, more than any woman before.

He slapped his thighs. The time had come to do something about this. But he wasn't ready to make amends.

More than anything, he wanted to pull his hair out. Realizing that it probably was not the best idea to continue this show of emotions in a public parking lot, he opened his door and slid into the driver's seat.

His phone rang. The caller ID showed his editor's name. "Good afternoon, Anne."

"How did the story go?"

"Great. I pulled a lot of original quotes."

"That's my star reporter. Are you on your way back to work now?"

"Yes."

"Good. Meet me in my office as soon as you return. I have something important to discuss with you."

Could it be? Maybe Anne wanted to offer him

the promotion? "I'll be there."

Chapter 13

Beep! Beep! Beep!

Traci hit her alarm clock and rolled out of bed with a thump. She groaned.

7:00 a.m. on a weekend morning. She rubbed her eyes and tried to remember why she'd set her alarm so early.

Right. She promised Carla that she'd go to church because Carla thought that it would make her feel better. Traci yawned. She wasn't used to waking up this early on a day off. But she had an hour to make herself presentable before Carla picked her up for the one-hour drive to her church in Alexandria, Virginia.

Why Carla, who lived across town from Traci, chose to drive so far to church every week in another state was beyond her reasoning. Carla must really love her church.

On Friday, she noted Traci's sadness and said she knew just what would cheer her. A sermon about relationships. She believed Traci, who hadn't been to church since her ex-fiancé left her at the altar, should hear it.

After five minutes of hearing Carla gush about her church's welcoming atmosphere and legendary pastor who preached good, Bible-based sermons, Traci finally gave in and agreed. To keep her from bailing, Carla told Traci that she'd pick her up at eight.

She glanced at the clock. Carla was right. If she wasn't going to drive her to church today, she'd go back to bed and sleep until noon.

~

Marc trailed behind Victor, who set a brisk pace ahead of him. He turned around. "Man, if you want a good seat in the sanctuary, you better walk faster."

Why had he allowed Victor to convince him to visit his church in Alexandria today? Oh, yeah. He said something about it having a legendary pastor whose sermons were on-point and that the pastor's sermon today was about relationships.

Victor stood at the front entrance, pausing to glare at Marc who still shuffled along. He quickened his pace. The cool, early November breeze refreshed him, and as he approached the entrance, he almost wished he could linger longer outside, just to enjoy the crisp air.

The greeter at the door, a petite woman whose blue dress peeked out beneath her black coat, extended her hand toward Marc. "Good morning, and happy Sabbath."

Marc shook the woman's hand. "Good morning."

"Is this your first time visiting Community Praise Center?"

Victor reached out and slapped Marc on his back. "He's with me."

The woman handed him a bulletin. "Any friend of Victor's is a friend of mine. Welcome to CPC. Enjoy the service."

Victor and Marc entered the church, and the sound of the greeter welcoming the next people as they approached the entrance reached him. He waited until he and Victor were out of earshot to talk. "Another woman who likes you."

Victor widened his eyes. "Who?"

Marc nodded in the direction of the entrance.

"Oh, Susie? She's a sweetheart, but nah, she's not my type."

"What is your type, Victor?"

"The type that's not your type, which is why we get along so well."

Marc chuckled. He and Victor never fought over women, because their taste in them was so different. Victor liked those who were fashionable, had curly hair, and stick-thin bodies. Marc liked women who were healthy, happy, and intriguing. All of his ex-girlfriends fit that type at first.

But then there was Traci. He would never meet another girl who was better than her. Should he apologize? Try to mend their relationship? How could they ever restore trust?

Her dishonesty cut him. Though he tried to start a conversation at the press conference, he didn't know if they could move on from here. Besides, Traci didn't want to talk about it. Not after he ignored her calls and text messages.

They entered the sanctuary, and he took in his

surroundings. Women dressed to the nines in beautiful outfits, high heels, and two-piece suits chatted with others who wore elaborate hats.

None of the men wore jeans. They all dressed in sharp suits and shiny shoes. He tugged on his preppy green sweater and made a mental note to wear a sports jacket next time. Not that there would be a next time. His visit to Victor's church was going to be a one-time deal unless Providence said otherwise.

He followed his friend to the front row of the church and slid into the seat next to him. When Victor started talking with the woman sitting to his left, Marc took the opportunity to glance at the church bulletin. He raised his eyebrows as he read the sermon title. The Broken Road. The title of the featured song was "Bless the Broken Road." He hoped this wasn't going to be a sentimental homily.

A glint of sunlight on honey-blonde hair caught his eye. His heartbeat sounded in his ears.

Traci.

She was a vision of pure beauty. She wore a brown skirt, green leggings, black knee-high boots, and a green sweater. Her bright smile highlighted her beautiful, almost-make-up-free face as she spoke to the lady next to her in the pew.

Victor elbowed him in the ribs. "You okay?"

He gulped. He couldn't help but gape at her.

Victor leaned over. "Who are you staring at?"

"Traci. She's here."

"Who is she sitting with?"

"I don't know. But she's across the aisle, wearing a green sweater."

"Wow, she's beautiful. Looks like a sweet girl."

"I could not agree with you more."

"Go talk to her."

"I can't. I haven't returned her calls. And she didn't want to talk to me when we ran into each last week."

"So, go do it anyway, man. It's not rocket science."

"No. Not here. Not now."

"Have it your way."

~

Traci had just opened her bulletin when Carla nudged her right arm. "Don't look now, but I think the love of your life is here. I recognize him from the picture on your desk."

Traci took in a sharp breath. "Marc."

"Um yeah, and he's with a good-looking guy. You need to introduce me after church service is over."

Her midsection tightened. "Carla, I can't."

"Why not?"

"Marc and I aren't together anymore. Remember?"

Carla let out a chortle. "You two are so still together. You're just having a lover's spat."

Traci's fanned her hot face with the program.

"If you won't introduce me to your boyfriend's friend, then I'll introduce myself. And I'll march you right over there with me. So what's it going to be?"

Traci bit her bottom lip. "Fine."

Carla gave Traci's right arm a reassuring squeeze.

The sound of music filled the sanctuary. A lady in a sharp suit and feathered hat took center stage and asked the congregation to stand for the call to worship. Everyone rose to their feet. Like a conductor, the lady directed them in the classic hymn, "My Hope Is Built on Nothing Less".

The music stirred something in Traci's soul. Something she almost forgot. Could it be hope?

She glanced at Marc seated across from her. Maybe there was hope for their broken trust. Maybe God would restore their relationship. But there was only one way to know for sure.

They had to talk.

Chapter 14

Traci and Marc walked beside each other out of church as Victor and Carla trailed a few paces behind. Traci made good on her word to introduce her coworker to Marc and Victor after the church service concluded.

She gazed back. Carla chatted with Victor, who let out a chortle. Before they walked out of the parking lot on their way to the Mexican restaurant, Carla's right arm was looped through Victor's left. She focused all her attention on him, smiling and even winking. He leaned over and whispered in her ear.

A little ache settled in Traci's stomach. She had that same connection with Marc. She glanced at him. He stared at the sidewalk. At least she used to have that same connection with him.

Why did they agree to do lunch after church today? He couldn't even look at her. He didn't hold her hand or pull her close.

The smell of chilies and warm corn tortillas

wafted on the air as they approached the restaurant. Good. She was famished and her feet ached after that twenty-minute walk, even though she wore boots that didn't usually pinch her feet. She glanced at Carla. She sported flats. Sensible girl.

Marc held open the heavy wood door. She muttered a thank you as she passed under the brick arch. He nodded. It was the most communication they'd had since their awkward and tense meeting at the educator's awards ceremony.

A petite hostess with a perky grin met them as they approached her station. She scooped four menus into her arms and spoke to Traci. "Table for four?"

Victor broke his conversation with Carla to step in. "A booth, please. We like it cozy." He winked at Carla. She giggled.

The shivers reverberated through Traci. Sitting in a booth meant Carla would cuddle with Victor, and she would be sitting close to Marc. Too close for someone who was still too upset to speak.

The hostess nodded. "Follow me."

The company of four shadowed her to a booth on the right side of the restaurant, only a few steps from the bathroom. Perfect. She'd probably need to retreat to there to gather her nerves and calm down.

Carla slipped into one side of the booth, and Victor slid in next to her. Marc stood still. Traci didn't move. No way was she going to be trapped between him and the wall. She had to be on the outside for an easy exit.

Carla shook her head. "Are you two going to have a seat?"

Ah, now she could talk to Marc by addressing Carla. "I just prefer to sit on the outside. I get kind of claustrophobic in booths."

Marc sighed and shuffled in. She scooted in beside him. Her left shoulder touched his right arm. She slid away from him, across the sticky vinyl so that she almost hung off the edge of the seat. As far from Marc as possible.

Carla frowned. "Excuse me, Victor. But I need to go freshen up. And I need you to come with me, Traci."

Victor nodded. He allowed Carla a smooth exit.

Once they both stood, Carla grabbed Traci by the arm and led her to the ladies' room. She pulled her to the fancy vanity mirror area of the restroom and hissed at Traci. "What is wrong with you?"

Traci brushed a tear that escaped her eye. Her bottom lip quivered. "Marc doesn't love me anymore."

Carla's face relaxed. She reached out and rubbed Traci's arms. "Oh honey, he loves you. I still see it in his eyes."

Traci let out a short laugh. "Really? He barely looks at me anymore."

"We're going to pray about this, and we're going to go back out there, and you two are going to work this out. Maybe not today, but I have full faith that you two will be on good terms again, because honey, the same God that brought you together can keep you together."

"We're going to pray now?"

Carla nodded and surveyed the stalls. "No one's here but us. So I'm going to pray aloud."

Traci closed her eyes.

"Dear God. Please open the hearts of Traci and Marc in a wonderful way that will endear them to each other again. Help them to move past their conflict and restore their relationship to everything you want it to be. Answer the deepest desires of their hearts and bless them, please. In Jesus' name I pray. Amen."

Sobs tore at Traci. Carla hugged her. "Everything will be all right." She reached for the tissue box on the counter by the vanity mirrors. Traci took it and wiped her eyes.

"I'm going out there." Carla turned to leave, then glanced over her shoulder. "You return when you're ready. But try to get back before we leave, okay? Don't hide out here."

A laugh escaped Traci. She smiled and nodded. Carla knew her so well. She did want to hunker down in here until it was time to go home.

She examined herself in the mirror. Black streaks of mascara marred her face. Good thing she hadn't worn any other makeup. She wiped her face clean and reached into her purse for her mascara wand but paused. One of the many things that she loved about Marc was that he didn't care if she wore makeup. He appreciated her natural look.

If only he would show her that he still loved her and everything was going to be okay. She took a deep breath. Carla's prayer replayed in her mind. She set the tissue box down. Little by little, she allowed the air to escape her lungs.

I trust you, Lord.

She mustered her best smile. She would quit

hiding and return to Marc's side.

~

Marc excused himself from the table and walked across the red Saltillo tiles toward the men's restroom, the tang of cilantro in the air. When he approached the door, he bumped into Carla on her way out of the ladies' restroom.

"Excuse me," Carla said.

"I'm sorry."

Carla stopped. She stood before Marc and crossed her arms. She tilted her head to the right and scowled. "I hope you know that you're breaking her heart. Traci was going to tell you about the inheritance letter. She waited because she didn't want to lose you. That woman loves you. Really, truly loves you. She'd marry you in a heartbeat, even if there was no inheritance."

"But, there is. And how convenient that she had me around when she lost her job. All she has to do is get me to the chapel, and she'll solve her problems."

"Didn't you hear what I just said? Her love for you has nothing to do with money. She wants you, not the cash."

Marc kept quiet. He knew better than to get into an argument with Traci's best friend. Besides, who was she to get involved? This situation was between him and Traci.

Carla's head tilted further. She opened her mouth to speak, but then shut it and walked off with a huff.

This was going to make an interesting lunchtime now that not one but two women were mad at him. He glanced at his watch. Maybe he should leave early. He shook his head. He would wait it out. For now.

Five minutes later, he returned to his seat at the table. His heart flipped when Traci approached the booth a minute later. She must have been crying. She'd covered it up well, but she didn't have any more mascara on. Running makeup happened to Gina, too, when she wept. And he was sure he caused Traci's grief.

He wanted to kick himself. But it was so hard for him to move past her secret.

She settled in next to him, playing with the napkin-wrapped utensils, spinning them around and around. Victor and Carla hid behind the oversized menu. He perused his.

Traci rubbed the edge of hers. "Did you all order?"

Victor and Carla peered over their menu and spoke in unison. "No." They laughed.

Carla sat back. "It's like our minds are connected." She gazed at Victor.

He grasped her hand. "It's not the only thing about us that's connected." He winked, then kissed her fingers.

Carla blushed. "You're such a flirt."

"You're such a beautiful woman."

The color of Carla's face resembled that of the salsa on the table.

Had he and Traci been like that? Would they have such a relationship again? Her hands trembled. Was she nervous? Frightened?

He reached out and gave her hand a reassuring squeeze, then turned his attention to her. For the first time all day, her features relaxed. No lines of tension in her forehead. No scrunching of her brows. Without words, she thanked him.

Warmth flooded his heart. Traci was not the type of woman to rule a man by her emotions. Could her tears and her concern be real? Could he believe what Carla said about Traci's feelings for him?

Maybe they needed to talk. He scanned the room, abuzz with conversation. Not here. He leaned in and whispered to her. "Can we chat tomorrow, just the two of us?"

"Sure."

"I'll text you the address to the restaurant tonight."

She nodded.

Carla stared at him. His reporter instinct told him she knew something about their relationship. Hopefully, she was on his side despite their showdown earlier by the restroom.

Victor interrupted his thoughts. "The fish taco sounds good. What are you having, Marc?"

"Chicken enchiladas."

Traci piped up. "Me too."

"I'll have a fruit salad," Carla said. "This girl's got to watch her figure."

Victor leaned in. "You're beautiful just the way you are."

She giggled as Victor kissed her hand again.

Traci leaned over Marc's menu and pointed at the picture of the grande nachos. Their arms touched. Electricity shot through him. Was his heart still beating?

Chapter 15

Marc sat in the comfort of his car. Yet squirmed in the seat as he gazed at the restaurant within view of his position in the parking lot. He glanced at his watch. It was five minutes after seven. He was five minutes late to his meeting with Traci.

He couldn't see her from his car, but he was sure she was already there. Knowing how much she valued promptness, she'd probably arrived early.

A heavy sigh escaped Marc's body. He wasn't ready. His heart still hurt from her dishonesty. He didn't know if he could find it in him to forgive her. Yet something about her made him want to give their relationship a second chance. He just didn't know if he could do this today.

A loud ring alerted him, startling him and jolting him out of his thoughts. Just his cell phone. He reached for it. "Hello?"

"Hola amigo! Where you at?"

It was Victor.

"I'm here at a restaurant." Should he tell Victor

any details? Maybe he should. After all, Victor was the one who helped him start this relationship.

"I'm meeting with Traci."

"Aw, man. Go ahead in there and tell her that you love her! I'm hanging up."

"Victor, wait. I don't know if this is a good idea. What do you—."

Marc held the phone away from his ear as the dial tone buzzed. It was now or never. He slipped his phone into his jacket pocket, squared his shoulders, and made his way toward the restaurant entrance.

As he approached, he spied a floral shop next door. He'd buy a red rose. What woman didn't love them? He needed an icebreaker. That would be it.

~

Traci swirled her strawberry smoothie with the tall red straw. She glanced at her watch. Five minutes after seven. Five minutes after Marc said he'd meet her at the bistro. Maybe he was working on a tight deadline. They both were in the news business. It happened.

Maybe he wouldn't show up.

She took a sip, the sweet berry drink chilling her. She shivered.

Men in business suits, women in workout clothes, and kids in school uniforms filed in for dinner. Only the conversations of the wait staff with customers and the bustle and hustle of the servers moving in and out the kitchen rivaled the sound of people talking. Soft music with Italian lyrics played in the background.

She closed her eyes and swayed to the tune. So

beautiful. She'd love to live in Italy someday. Her cell phone's ringtone interrupted her private moment. She opened her eyes and answered it.

"Hello?"

"Good day. Is this Traci Hightower?"

"Yes."

"This is Don Herald from the *Annapolis Record* newspaper. We received your résumé."

Traci perked up. She'd started her job search a few days after receiving her two weeks' notice. Could it be that one of the first places she applied to was interested? "Yes, I remember sending it to you. Thanks for getting back to me."

There was a brief pause. She didn't breathe.

"You have a good résumé, Ms. Hightower, and engaging clips. However, we chose another candidate who was a better fit."

Her breath rushed from her lungs, but she did her best to maintain a professional tone. "Thank you for letting me know."

"You're welcome. Good luck on your job search."

The dial tone sounded in her ears before she could respond. Tears welled in her eyes. She placed her phone on the table and reached for a napkin. As she wiped her eyes, she heard a gentle, kind, and very familiar voice. One she had missed so much.

"Hey, Trace."

Her heart came to a standstill as she refocused her eyes from her phone to Marc. He held a single red rose. Moisture gathered in the corners of her eyes as he extended the flower to her.

"This is for you."

She came to her feet and accepted the bloom, inhaling the sweet aroma. "Oh, Marc, thank you. It's beautiful."

He sat down in the chair across from her, his forehead crinkled. "Is everything okay?"

She wiped the tears from her eyes. "Yes. Why?"

He paused for a beat. "You seem sad."

"Since I was let go, I decided to start looking for a new place of employment. The phone call that I just took was a potential employer. He said that while my résumé and newspaper clips were impressive, they found a better fit to hire."

He shook his head. The lines around his eyes softened. "I'm sorry."

She peered at him over the rose. "I owe you an apology."

"Traci—"

"No, please, let me finish. It's why I've been calling you, and why I wanted to meet with you. Even if you never find it in your heart to forgive me, I need to say the words."

He placed his napkin on his lap. Was that an indication that he meant to stay and at least hear her out?

Her heart now beat a furious tempo. "I want to apologize for not telling you about the inheritance earlier. It's just that . . . I was so scared you'd leave me and when you walked out, I thought, I thought we were over. And then when you didn't call me, I thought I'd lost you."

"I'm sorry, Trace. I should have returned your calls, but your dishonesty hurt me. I've been burned too many times by ex-girlfriends who couldn't tell the truth. I thought you were different. And then you dropped that bomb on me. Right after you told me you'd lost your job. What was I supposed to think?"

He was going to walk out on her. "You're right. Honesty in a relationship is everything. My ex wasn't up-front with me, either. I know how it feels to be lied to. I never meant to keep it from you. But the timing was all wrong. I lost my job. How could I tell you then?"

"And I do appreciate that you wanted to tell me." He twirled his spoon. "I want to forgive you."

"But you can't."

"I'm working on it. Forgiveness, healing, and trust will all take time. Do you understand?"

"Are you saying you're willing to work things out?"

"I'm sorry for walking out on you that night at your apartment. I should never have left you like that."

"You don't need to apologize. I'm the one in the wrong."

"As long as you realize this isn't a guarantee, I'd like to see what happens from here. It's going to take time. And a commitment from both of us to be up front with each other from now on."

"I promise." She blinked to make sure he was real.

He reached across the table and touched her hand. "Then, I'm willing to give our relationship another chance."

The look in his coffee-brown eyes sent her heart into somersaults. If they were not in the middle of a restaurant filled with onlookers, she would have wanted to stay in this moment forever.

But another issue hung in the air between them. She bit her lip.

Marc frowned. "What's wrong?"

"We need to discuss my inheritance."

"Okay."

"I wanted to tell you I know how I would have used the money. If I'd ever gotten it."

"Go on."

"I would've established my own bookstore and called it Hallee's House after my cousin. She was like a sister to me. She died from cancer before she reached her teenage years."

"I'm sorry to hear that."

Traci bit the inside of her cheek. "We dreamed of opening our own place one day. We wanted to share our love for literature with the world."

He leaned in. "That's a great idea. You should go for it."

She smiled. "It's kind of hard to start a business without money." Her heart beat like she'd run a marathon as she reached into her purse and pulled out the inheritance letter.

With trembling hands, she ripped it into shreds. "I choose you over that money, Marc."

He widened his eyes. "Why did you do that?"

"To prove to you that the inheritance means nothing to me if I don't have you in my life."

For a moment, he stared at her. Had she just blown it? What was going on in his brain? "Penny for your thoughts?"

He winked. "You can't afford my thoughts."

Before she could say anything, he got up, moved to her side of the table, and kissed her cheek.

Her heart pounded even faster.

Maybe there was hope for their relationship to be restored.

Chapter 16

Marc strolled into the newspaper office, whistling. The meeting with Traci went better than he expected. He believed her apology and her promise not to lie anymore.

Victor crossed his path. "Good, you're here. Anne wants to see you."

Was his day about to get even better? He headed past his cubicle and toward Anne's office. He knocked on the door.

"It's open."

He stepped inside. "Good morning, Anne. You wanted to see me?"

His boss looked up from the stack of papers on her desk. She held her red pen in mid-air. "Yes, please have a seat."

He followed orders.

"You're from Chicago, correct?"

"Correct."

Anne grinned. "How would you like to go home and write for the *Chicago Reporter*?"

He gripped the edge of the chair. "Are you talking about the promotion we discussed last week?"

"The job is yours."

As a kid, he dreamed of writing for the *Reporter*. He begged his dad to drive by their office building every day, just so he could get a glimpse of what he believed was his future workplace. Now, years later, Anne handed him his heart's desire on a silver platter.

But what about Traci?

"I cannot read minds, Marc. Break the silence and speak. Do you want the job?"

"Yes. But I need to think about it first."

Anne tapped her pen on her desk. "You can think about it for one day. After that, I want a decision. My other reporters are lined up for this position. If you won't take it, I can assure you, someone else will."

"I understand." He stood.

"One day, Marc. I need to know by this time tomorrow or the job goes to someone else."

"Thank you, Anne. I'll be in touch."

He left the office and went to his cubicle. He sank into his chair and drew in a sharp breath. Little by little, he exhaled.

Dear God, what am I going to do? Traci and I are on good terms again. I love her. She loves me. I think she may be the one I want to marry. Life is good. But if I take this job in Chicago, what will that mean for my relationship with her?

~

Traci adjusted her makeup in the mirror. She

coated her lips with deep-rose lip gloss. She fluffed her hair and smiled at her reflection. Not bad for someone who just met a last-minute deadline in the office and rushed home in time to clean up her apartment and fix dinner for her date with her boyfriend.

Her heart tripped over itself. She had a boyfriend. A wonderful man who was unlike any one else she'd dated. Kind, caring, intelligent, God-fearing, and excellent at his job. Marc was Traci's dream guy.

Thank you, Jesus, for sending Marc to me. You've mended my broken heart with Your love and Marc's devotion. I couldn't ask for more.

A knock sounded at the door. She slipped her feet into flat, black ballerina slippers. She dressed on the comfortable side. Marc wasn't one to critique her outfits. He loved her heart and appreciated her just as she was. How wonderful to be loved without condition. It reminded her of how God loved everyone.

She rushed to her door and swung it open. Marc drew her in for a quick kiss. They parted ways, and she stepped aside. "Come in."

Marc entered and sniffed the air. "Something smells good."

"I tried cooking vegetarian lasagna and garlic bread. It's ready. We can eat now if you're hungry." She swiped her damp hands on her pants.

"Always. Let's eat."

~

Marc studied Traci as she enjoyed the hazelnut gelato she bought for dessert. He didn't want this to change. But he knew his news might make everything different.

She licked her spoon and peered at him out the corner of her eye. "What?"

"Nothing." He didn't know how to tell her.

She swallowed the last bite of ice cream and placed her spoon down. "We promised each other no more secrets. Spill it."

"I don't have a secret."

She smirked. "We're both talented journalists. I believe that you and I know when we're on the verge of a story."

He exhaled. "There is something that I need to tell you."

She sat back, her hands folded. "Go ahead. I'm listening."

He studied her for a few seconds before speaking. He prayed that this would not end their evening on a negative note. "My editor offered me my dream job earlier today."

Her smile bloomed like a flower. "What wonderful news. Congratulations."

"It's in Chicago."

She leaned forward. "As in Illinois?"

He nodded.

She glanced at her hands then back up at him before speaking in a quiet voice. "Are you going to take it?"

"I want to. But I don't want to leave you."

"It's not fair to use me as a roadblock to your dreams."

Marc stood. "Roadblock? You are a blessing, not a roadblock."

"If you want this job, Marc, you should take it. I'll be fine."

He closed the distance between them and went to touch her.

She moved out of his reach. "I don't want to be the person who stopped you from pursuing your passion. You'd grow to regret me."

"Trace, you're thinking too far ahead."

"Didn't I have reason to think far ahead?"

"Yes."

"What is this? Where is our relationship headed? Because if you don't see me in your future, then why are you even hesitating to take this new job?"

He reached out again. She stepped to the side.

He rubbed his chin. "Because, it's in Chicago, and that's too far away from you."

"What do you want?"

"I want you. And this job. Can't I have both?"

Her tense shoulders relaxed a tiny bit. "You're suggesting a long-distance relationship?"

He closed the gap between them. This time, she did not move. He drew her close and brushed a wisp of hair out of her angelic-looking face. "If you're willing to try, I am too."

Tears pooled in her eyes. She melted. "I'm willing."

Marc kissed her. Slow, deep, and tender.

Chapter 17

Traci set three fall-foliage illustrated placemats on the fine oak dining room farm table inside her parents' hacienda in Santa Fe, California, the aroma of pumpkin pie and green bean casserole reaching her nose. Thanksgiving fell at just the right time. She needed a good visit and her mother's restaurant-quality cooking. It was also good to get away from things she was dealing with in Maryland.

She paused after placing the third plate onto the table. "Mom?"

Her mom peeked around the corner from the kitchen. "Yes?"

"Is it just you, Dad, and me this Thanksgiving?"

"Yes."

When she finished, she sat on a stool in the kitchen to watch her mom cook. With a professional chef for a mother, she was never hungry because there was always food, good food, for breakfast, lunch, dinner, and the in between. "You know, most of my best memories revolve around food. The smells from the kitchen remind me of my childhood. I've always loved to watch you move around. It's like a dance for you."

"That's sweet of you to say." Mom stirred something in a bubbling pot on the stove. "But you're troubled. Last night, you picked at your dinner. That's not like you. What's going on?"

"You don't want to know."

"Try me."

Traci played with the edges of the brown and orange cloth that covered the kitchen island counter. "I miss Marc."

"I know. You called me every week after you started dating him to gush about how wonderful he was. It's only natural now that he's moved to another state that you miss him."

"Several states away."

Mom stirred the pumpkin puree for the mini-tarts. The cinnamon and clove scent tickled Traci's nose and set her stomach to rumbling.

"Have you reached out to him since he left?"

"Yes. He calls me almost every night. We've had some great conversations."

Mom didn't say a word or look up from stirring the puree in the pot.

"I don't know if this long-distance relationship will work for us. I need him near me."

Mom nodded, intent on dessert.

"I'm happy that he landed his dream job. It's a great accomplishment for his journalism career. He's no longer struggling or paying his dues. That's good for him. But Mom, I miss him. The daily phone calls are not the same as actual dates, like when he's here in person. What should I do?"

Mom stopped stirring. "I can't tell you what to do, honey. You need to make that decision. But I can tell you that if you and Marc are meant to be together, God will work it out for you."

"I hope you're right. I really do."

Traci sighed and slunk into a chair at the kitchen table. Mom looked up from stirring the pot. "There's more, isn't there?"

"I lost my job."

Mom stopped stirring. "Oh, dear. How did that happen?"

Traci explained the situation to her mom. After listening to her story, Mom sighed.

"Exactly how I feel," Traci said. "I loved my job despite the insufficient salary."

Mom walked over to the table and gave her daughter a hug. She stroked her hair. "God will provide."

Traci nestled against her mom. Her hugs always provided comfort.

"Maybe you should consider moving back home."

Traci pulled away. "I can't do that. I'm twenty-seven years old. And I don't want to strain your own budget."

Mom chuckled. "So? You're still our child, and we want to make sure that you have a roof over your head. Or are you telling me you can still manage to pay your rent for your apartment?"

Traci shifted on the stool. "No. My lease is up in December. I only have money to pay that."

"Well, it's settled then." Mom wiped her hands on her apron as if that closed the conversation.

"What is?"

"Your father and I will fly to Maryland and help you pack. You rent the moving truck, and we'll drive across country back home to California before the New Year. We can fly in two weeks before Christmas and have you home in time for the holidays."

It would be great to have someone look out for her again. "I do miss home. Maybe I could look for a job here and stay until I get back on my feet."

Mom cupped Traci's chin. "That's my girl." She kissed Traci's right cheek, and then returned to cooking.

What would she do without her parents? They always were there for her and took care of her when she needed it. Maybe she would land a job in journalism here in California. Then again, she would be back to being the low man on the ladder, paying her dues. She grimaced.

Maybe she'd get a job at a restaurant. Her mother had connections, and Traci loved being around food. Plus, the industry was very lucrative.

A booming voice sliced through the moment of silence. "When do we eat?"

Traci grinned. Her dad was always ready to partake of Mom's cooking. He sauntered into the kitchen, encircled his wife's waist, and held her tight as he stood behind her. He kissed her cheek. Mom giggled like a schoolgirl and swatted away his advances.

This was the kind of relationship she wanted.

And she wanted it with Marc. Could they have it when he lived a thousand miles away from her? She pulled out her cell phone.

Mom went back to assembling the tarts. "Meal time is family time. No technology allowed. You may be grown, but the rules haven't changed."

"Yes, Mom." She hopped off of the barstool. "I'm just going to step outside. I'll be back."

As she left the room, Mom giggled again. Traci's heart ached. She'd give anything to have Marc here, not with his family in Chicago.

She brushed the dust on the veranda with her brown leather cowgirl boots and sat in the swinging chair. The scent of pollution-free, pine-scented air rejuvenated her senses. Marc should be here to experience this.

She pulled up his number and pressed the call button. He answered after the first ring. "Happy Thanksgiving, love."

"Happy Thanksgiving to you too."

"How's the weather in the California countryside?"

"Perfect, as always."

"I'll have to get out there sometime."

"Yes, you definitely should." She kicked at a stone. "How's the weather in the Windy City?"

"Cold."

She chuckled.

"It would be much warmer if you were here with me."

"Or if you sat on this swing beside me."

"You could move to Chicago. You don't have a job tying you down to Maryland."

True, she didn't, but she wasn't going to chase him halfway across the country without a commitment. She didn't even have enough money to put gas in her car at this point. And no job prospects in Chicago. She couldn't pay rent there, either. "I don't think that would work. I don't know what I'm going to do. I'd like to stay in Maryland, but I might move home and consider my options."

A hint of resignation tinged his voice. "You'd leave the place you love?"

"You aren't there anymore."

The two chatted until Mom called her for dinner. She glanced at her watch. One hour flew by in what felt like five minutes. Like always. "I have to go."

"Tell your parents I said hello."

"I will."

"Take care, love."

"Take care, handsome."

Traci ended the call. How much longer could she endure this?

Chapter 18

Traci flipped through the pages of *Hope's Fire*, a contemporary romance written by Marc's sister Gina. She hadn't been able to stop reading since she started.

She glanced at the clock. 8:30. She'd skipped dinner because the story was so good that she wasn't even hungry. A yawn escaped her. Who was she kidding? She was going to lose valuable sleep tonight, and she didn't even care, because the book was that well written.

Just as she resumed reading, her cell phone rang. Who was interrupting? According to caller ID, her best friend. She answered the phone. "Hey, Carla."

"Hey, there. I miss you at work. How are you?"

Traci glanced around her bedroom from the comfortable position under the covers of her bed where she sat with two oversized pillows against the headboard. The view was one she'd enjoyed her entire childhood. She was looking forward to relocating. "I'm doing great. Still at my parent's house."

"In California?"

"Yes, ma'am."

"Lucky! Such beautiful weather, right?"

"Always."

"Are you staying there forever? Or returning to Maryland?"

Traci peered at the calendar on her wall. She'd been home for one full week after Thanksgiving. "My parents and I are going to fly to Maryland in a few days to pack my belongings and drive a moving truck to California."

"Oh."

"Oh? You sound sad."

"Yes, girl. I'm sad because I'm going to miss you and our fun times together."

"I'll miss you too. But you're welcome to visit me in Cali."

"I'll think about it. That would be nice. So, what are you reading?"

Traci frowned. "How do you know that I'm reading?"

"You sounded a bit annoyed when you answered the phone, like I was interrupting a good book."

Traci laughed. "I'm reading *Hope's Fire*. Marc's sister wrote it."

"I didn't know she was an author."

Traci smoothed over the gold seal on the back cover of the book. "Gina is an award-winning author of inspirational romance."

"Wow."

"What?"

"That Marc man of yours is really helping you

get closer to God, isn't he?"

"What do you mean?"

"Five months ago, you wouldn't consider reading any book in your free time that was inspirational or talked about God."

Traci sat back against the pillows. "You're right."

"You need to marry this guy."

What a dream. "Why?"

"He's good for you. He treats you like a lady, he loves God, and his loving you is helping you love God more."

The lump in her throat reduced her ability to inhale. Carla was right. She was blessed. But, even though Marc loved her, he lived so far away.

"If he doesn't propose by this time next year, you better."

"Carla!"

"Just kidding, girl. The man should propose, always."

Traci twisted the edge of the blanket.

"Everything okay?"

Did she dare say the words out loud? "I don't know if this long-distance relationship is going to work."

"Why not?"

"He's in Chicago, a thousand miles away from me. I miss having him with me. I miss his hugs. I miss his kisses. I miss his smile."

"Okay, I get the point. Spare me the mushy details, please. Remember, I'm still a single lady. Don't make me jealous. Here's what you need to do. Call Marc and tell him how you feel."

"We already talked about this."

"And how did that go?"

"He doesn't want to leave Chicago, and though I'm leaving Maryland for California, I don't see myself relocating to Chicago just to be with him when we're not married and committed to each other legally. Plus, there's the matter of me not having a job."

"That's tough. All I can tell you, Traci, is that if God wants for you and Marc to be together, He will work it out for you."

The exact words her Mom used.

Traci peered heavenward. *God, is this confirmation that there's hope for my relationship with Marc?*

~

Traci woke up with the book, *Hope's Fire*, open and resting on her lap. She stretched, yawned, and grimaced. Her back hurt from sleeping in a sitting position. She removed the book from her lap, tumbled out of bed, and rubbed her eyes. Why was it so bright?

She stared at the clock. Ten? Her heart raced. She was late for work. Within moments, she opened the dresser drawer to pull out a shirt. Oh, wait a minute. She didn't have a job anymore. And she was in California.

After grabbing a cup of coffee from the kitchen, she picked up the book from her bed and smiled. It had been a very good read from start to finish.

Maybe Gina would like to hear how much she'd enjoyed it. Traci woke up her computer and searched for Gina's Facebook page. She clicked

"Add Friend" and saw the automatic response, "Friend Request Sent." Before she could blink twice, Gina had accepted her request.

Traci stared at the screen. Was she really doing this? Reaching out to Marc's sister to be friends? Could Gina help her get Marc to trust her again? There was only one way to find out. Traci sent a private message to Gina's inbox.

Hey, Gina! This is Traci. Your brother Marc is our mutual friend. We're dating. I loved your book Hope's Fire*! Read it from cover to cover last night. I was wondering if we could talk?*

Traci reached for her mug and took several long sips of her coffee while she awaited Gina's response. Five minutes and an empty coffee mug later, Gina sent a response.

Traci! I've heard so much about you from Marc. Yes, we can talk. Is now a good time? If so, call me.

Traci set her empty mug down and reached for her cell phone. Here went nothing. She dialed Gina's number.

"Good morning! Gina speaking."

Traci paused. Had this been a good idea?

"Hello?"

"Hey, Gina. This is Traci."

"Traci! Yes, hi. How are you?"

Traci ran her free hand across the smooth, cherry wood desk. "I'm okay. How are you?"

"Wonderful. Getting a few chapters written

before my kids wake up. Marc said you met Samantha and Regan, right?"

Traci smiled. "Yes, I have. Your children are delightful!"

Gina chuckled. "I agree. So, what did you want to talk about?"

"Well, I read your book, *Hope's Fire,* and enjoyed it so much."

"Thank you, hun. I love it when readers love my books. A lot of work and sleepless nights go into each one."

Traci bit her bottom lip.

"But I have a feeling it's not my book that you want to talk about." Gina took the words out of Traci's mouth. "Is this about my brother?"

"Yes."

"Go ahead, talk. I'm listening."

Traci confided in Gina about how much she cared for Marc and why she and Marc fought. She shared that she didn't think that Marc fully forgave her and didn't trust her.

"Well Traci, I can tell you that Marc loves you. Some of his girlfriends really hurt him, so that's why he's finding it hard to forgive you completely. But I think I know what may help."

Traci perked up. "Really? What?"

"When Marc and I were children, our parents instilled within us a knowledge and love for God. Growing up, we each had our favorite Bible verses. I had hundreds, but the one Marc always leaned on and went to was Jeremiah 29:11. I think that, deep in his heart, he still treasures that verse and will return to it when his future seems uncertain. Kind of like now."

Traci wanted to cheer. She knew just what she was going to get Marc for Christmas.

Chapter 19

Christmas music by Nat King Cole sounded throughout Gina's townhouse. Marc and his parents had flown in from Chicago to spend the holiday with Gina and her children. The spicy scent of gingerbread cookies mixed with sweet fragrance of homemade peppermint bark and the savory aroma of a turkey that had been cooking for hours.

"Mom!" Gina called from the kitchen. "Do you think the turkey's ready?"

Marc relaxed on the plush, evergreen-colored couch as his mom rushed into the kitchen to assist. It was the first Christmas Gina had hosted. He'd teased her about messing up the turkey, but maybe he made her nervous.

He tapped his foot on the floor to the tune of *Deck the Halls* that was next on the Nat King Cole playlist. "Hurry up in the kitchen. I can't wait much longer."

Gina peeked out the door and huffed, a wooden spoon in her hand. "Impatient children don't get a slice of pumpkin pie."

"I'll be sure to tell the kids."

His sister shook her head, and then disappeared into the kitchen.

From the family room came the sounds of the kids laughing. How good to hear such cheer in Gina's house again. It had been a long time.

An older man's deep bellow sounded over theirs. A smile spread across Marc's face. His dad was entertaining Samantha and Regan. Since moving to Chicago, Marc missed his niece and nephew more than he thought he would.

Without warning, Samantha rushed into the living room. She spotted Marc, grinned, and bounded into his lap. He caught her, and she gave him a hug before she pulled back to stare at him. "Uncle Marky, can we open our presents now?"

Marc chuckled. Before he could reply, Gina answered from the kitchen. "No, Samantha. You know the rules. We eat dinner first."

She pouted.

"I understand the feeling. Maybe if you ask your mom very nicely, she'll let you open a few."

Samantha nodded, jumped off of Marc's lap, and ran to the kitchen. "But Mom. Uncle Marky said to be nice and let us open some of them."

Marc shook his head. "Hey, wait a minute."

"Grandma, please."

Well played, Samantha.

Sure enough, his mother stepped in. "Well honey, the turkey won't be ready for another hour. We might as well open the presents now."

Regan rushed into the living room. "Mommy, we

can open them now?"

Gina followed Samantha in from the kitchen. "Fine."

The kids dove under the Christmas tree and wasted no time in unwrapping their gifts. Their sweet faces radiated pure delight as they opened present after present and jumped for joy as they pulled out each gift from its silver bell wrapping paper.

"Children are a gift from God, aren't they?"

Marc glanced at his dad who'd come to watch the commotion.

"Yes, they are."

Dad sat in a chair near Marc. He spoke so that only Marc could hear him. "Your Mom and I aren't getting any younger, son."

Marc frowned. "What do you mean?"

"Your mom doesn't want you to wait until you're too old to have kids to get married. She wants more grandchildren."

"We'll see." Could he trust Traci? Marriage was too big of a step to make a mistake.

Suddenly, Samantha was in his face. She extended a big, rectangular box. "Uncle Marky, this is for you."

"You got me a gift?"

Samantha shook her head. "It says, 'To Marc, from Traci.'"

Gina sat beside him. "Traci stopped by last week. She wanted you to have this before she relocated to California."

Marc nodded. He offered to help with the packing, but she refused him. Knowing she would be busy, he didn't stop by to visit. Hopefully their relationship wasn't going backward because of his refusal to completely forgive her. But this Christmas gift may be a sign that she was willing to wait for him. Right?

He removed the red sleigh-pattern wrapping paper and lifted the lid on the cardboard box to reveal a journaling Bible. Samantha and Regan, who were done with their presents, stood by.

Samantha leaned over Marc. "What is it?"

Marc ran his hand over the smooth, brown leather of his favorite book.

"It's a Bible."

"Ooo," Samantha said. "It's nice."

Traci had his name inscribed in gold on the bottom right corner of the cover. A bookmark stuck out from in between the pages. He pulled it out, counting eleven red roses drawn on it. Flipping it over, he found the words to Jeremiah 29:11.

His favorite Bible verse.

And those eleven roses. They signified that a person was truly, deeply loved. That came from one of his sister's books, the only one that he read, at her insistence.

He didn't move from his seat as everyone made their way to the dining room table.

He knew what he needed to do.

~

Marc sat on the couch in the living room. Everyone else in the house had gone to bed an hour ago. But he couldn't sleep.

He knew that he should completely forgive Traci. That's what the Lord called him to do. But forgiveness didn't come easily. And trust was even harder. He just needed guidance from God. His future hung in the balance, because while he loved Traci, her dishonesty still stung.

He opened the Bible Traci gave him with the nice, extra-wide white space in the margins of each page. A journaling Bible, perfect for the reporter in him as he loved to write and the doodler in him to draw on its crisp, white pages. Marc reached for a blue ink pen on the coffee table. Since he didn't have colorful markers on hand, this would do.

He turned to Jeremiah 29 where the bookmark still lay, and slowly underlined the text. He whispered the words. "'For I know the plans I have for you,' declares the Lord, 'plans to prosper you and not to harm you, plans to give you hope and a future.'"

He wrote in the margin. *Lord, I know that you have good plans for me. What is my future?*

No sooner than he had formed the question mark on the page than did God impress the answer on his heart.

Traci.

Chapter 20

Marc stepped out of his car, shut the door, and inhaled the clean, crisp mountain air that rejuvenated his senses. A beautiful hacienda sat in the center of a gorgeous, grassy yard that belonged to Traci's parents.

He jingled his keys before placing them into his right pants pocket. The little velvet box in the other pocket pressed against his leg as he made his way to the house. Stone-colored pebbles and sweet-scented flowers lined the walkway.

Marc paused as he stepped onto the porch and faced the front door. The porch swing creaked in the light breeze. That must be where Traci sat when they talked on the phone.

He drew a deep breath and said a silent prayer. God approved of what he was about to do. He'd prayed about this over Christmas and delved deep into the Bible for answers. He had a peace in his soul and a good word from God. This was the right step into that hope and future that the Lord promised him. He wiped his sweaty hands on his pants and rang the doorbell.

"I'm on my way!"

He chuckled at the sound of Traci's voice. Seconds later, she opened the door. Her jaw dropped open. Her eyes then lit up. She gasped and covered her mouth. In the next instant, she flung herself into his arms.

He caught her and held her. He'd missed her sweet smell of strawberries and cream.

"Marc! What are you doing here?"

He feigned a pout. "I'm happy to see you too."

She stepped back, her arms crossed. She tilted her head and pursed her lips. "So, you're not mad at me anymore?"

He shuffled his feet, first gazing at the porch floor, and then at the swing, before turning his attention to her. "Do you mind if we talk out here?"

She nodded and joined him on the swing. For a moment, they swayed in silence. He grasped her hand. But didn't look at her. Instead, they stared at the green pasture surrounding the home.

He inhaled a deep breath. "I'm sorry."

"Sorry for what?"

"For not trusting you. I did a lot of reflection over the Christmas holiday, and I realize that you didn't want to hurt me. I read that Bible you gave me as a gift. Thank you, by the way."

She nodded.

"And I realize that I don't want to be mad at you or have an unforgiving heart."

She turned away, but not before he saw a tear glistening on her cheek.

From this point on, he prayed that he would never be the cause of her sadness. He only wanted to bring her joy. Resolved that this would be a new beginning for the two of them, the start of something beautiful, he stood.

Then, he got down on one knee.

She gasped. "What are you …"

With a little squeak, he opened the little blue velvet box to reveal a sparkling diamond ring.

Her eyes widened. "Marc!"

The corners of his mouth tugged upward. "Traci Amanda Hightower, I love you deeper than the Pacific Ocean, wider than the span of all seven continents, higher than the clouds in the sky, and I would be honored if you would be my wife. Will you marry me?"

She rushed into his arms, knocking him off balance. They fell onto the cool concrete of the porch and laughed. Had two people ever been happier? She kissed him, and he kissed her back. He broke away to stare at the beautiful woman he hoped would accept his proposal. She beamed. He'd never seen a lovelier vision.

He held the ring toward her. "So, is that a yes?"

She extended her left hand. "Yes," she whispered. Marc echoed her silly grin as he slipped the diamond on her finger. For a moment, they just drank in being together.

Then, the front door clicked open, and a deep voice broke the silence. "What do we have here?"

Traci jumped to her feet and rushed into her parents' arms. "Mom, Dad, Marc wants to marry me. I'm engaged."

Traci's dad slapped his hands together. "Well, it's about time."

She swatted her dad's shoulder. "You knew."

"Of course I knew. Your man asked me for permission to marry you, just like any true gentlemen would. As you can see, I gave him my blessing."

"Thanks, Dad." She kissed his cheek.

Mom hugged her. "And I approve of him, one hundred percent."

"Thanks, Mom."

Her dad shook Marc's hand. "Welcome to the family, son."

"Thank you, sir. It is an honor."

Her dad led the way back into the house. "We're going to let you kids keep celebrating. Don't stay out too late."

Once the door shut, Marc reached for Traci's hands and clasped them. "I love you, Trace."

She closed the space between them and peered at him. "I love you, Marc."

They sealed their engagement with a passionate kiss.

~

Traci sat in a cushioned chair in a mahogany-line office next to her husband, waiting for Chadwick Morrison, their family lawyer, to speak. He examined their marriage certificate.

Two months after their honeymoon, they were stressed about not being able to pay all of their bills as they struggled to survive on Marc's income. She still hadn't found a job and didn't want to go back into journalism. So here they were, taking the inheritance they thought they wouldn't touch.

Celine Dion's song *Have You Ever Been in Love* played in the background. The first song that she and Marc danced to at their wedding reception. Two hundred of their closest friends and family filled in the seats of the Cascading Hills Mansion in Annapolis. She could still smell the smoked salmon with lemon and herb, the roasted potatoes, the baked chicken sautéed in mushroom sauce, the steamed broccoli, and the vegetarian lasagna. Her stomach growled.

"We can go eat after this meeting. I hear that you're hungry."

He rubbed her belly. She wasn't the only one hungry, but that news would have to wait.

Chadwick looked over his glasses at the couple. "Do you have a photo?"

Traci tugged on her shirt. "A photo?"

"Yes, from your wedding."

Marc whipped out his cell phone and showed Traci the image first. Their passionate kiss at the altar. "As a matter of fact, we do."

Marc handed his phone to Chadwick. He nodded. "Beautiful picture."

After he returned Marc's phone, Chadwick examined Henry Fort's will and retrieved a few papers from his briefcase. He pushed the papers across the desk and handed a pen to Traci. "Everything is clear and confirmed. And your mother has approved the match. Please sign on the lines I marked with an x."

Traci signed first, then Marc scribbled his signature on the paperwork. They pushed the papers back to Chadwick's side of the mahogany desk.

"Congratulations." He presented them with a cashier's check. "You are a very blessed couple."

Her hands trembling, Traci accepted the money. Marc leaned over to read it. His eyes grew as large as dinner plates.

She tried not to wrinkle the paper. "Chad, are you sure this isn't a mistake?"

"No. It is the exact amount your grandfather said to give you after you and your husband provided me with your marriage certificate."

Marc blew out a low breath. "Wow."

"Would you like for me to recommend a financial planner to help you two manage your new wealth?"

"Yes, please." Marc's voice held a note of incredulity.

Chadwick scribbled contact information for one of his colleagues and handed the paper to them. "Live well. I need to leave for another appointment."

They stood and shook hands with their lawyer. "Thank you."

"You are welcome."

Traci placed the check into her purse. They walked out of the office and went to their car in silence.

Marc pulled out of the parking lot. "That's enough money to live on until death do us part."

"I know." Her heart still hadn't resumed its normal rhythm. "It's enough for me to establish the bookstore that Hallee and I dreamed of."

"It's enough for me to hire an architect and

construction crew to build our dream house."

"It's enough for . . ." A wave of nausea overtook her. She covered her mouth.

Marc glanced at her. "Are you okay? Should I pull over?"

Traci nodded. He screeched to a stop on the side of the road just in time for Traci to swing open the car door and vomit onto the pavement. After a couple of minutes of upheaval, she closed the passenger door. Marc wiped her mouth and chin with a tissue.

"Sorry about that."

"I'm driving you to the ER. You've never been so sick."

She leaned back against the headrest. "No need to. They'll just tell us what I already know."

Marc's mouth dropped open into an O. "What do you know?"

"Seven months from now, we'll have new names. Mommy and Daddy."

He gasped. "You're pregnant?"

Traci nodded. "Confirmed yesterday by my doctor."

He pulled her close and kissed her temple. "This is wonderful news."

"At least we won't have to worry about diapers. Or a college fund."

"The Lord has provided at just the right time."

"That He did." She grimaced, swung the door open, and heaved.

"Let's get you home and get you feeling normal again."

"I have a feeling that nothing is going to be

normal anymore."

He slid the gear into drive and maneuvered the car back on the road. "Normal is overrated."

Epilogue

Traci gazed at the big blocks of yellow letters attached to the two-story, brown, brick-and-mortar building in the heart of downtown Chicago. Hallee's House. She turned to Marc. "I can't believe we're finally doing this."

He rubbed her lower back. "I can't believe we have twins."

"I believe that's a valid excuse to give Gina when she asks why we're late to our bookstore's grand opening and her book signing."

"Let's use it while we can."

She bent in front of the stroller and cooed at Matthew and Marianne. Matthew favored Marc with his dark hair and Marianne had her green eyes.

"Aw, Trace. Don't wake them up. Let's at least get inside the store and say hi to everyone first."

She stood. "You're right. I just love watching them while they sleep."

Marc held the door open for her as she pushed the stroller inside the building. The sweet scent of cupcakes and the calming aroma of coffee greeted her as she entered.

Dark brown carpet covered the entire first and second floors. She resisted the urge to take off her shoes and revel in the plush texture. The walls of the store were painted a pretty crème color. The shelves contained books from popular Christian authors, including inspirational fiction, Christian living books, autobiographies, and memoirs. The music section carried a wide variety of contemporary Christian and gospel music. It was part of the dream. To inspire people and point them to Jesus Christ.

Traci pushed the stroller around the store, taking in the sights and sounds of customers browsing and conversing. She waved at Carla, the general manager, and at Victor, the supervisor. They interacted well. There might just be another wedding in the works.

Could anyone be happier than her?

At the center of the store, Gina sat at the author table, chatting with customers and signing copies of her latest novel.

Traci sat down in the seat next to her. After signing a book and wishing the customer all the best, Gina engulfed Traci in a hug. "How's my favorite sister-in-law?"

"I'm your only sister-in-law."

Gina chuckled. "And I wouldn't have it any other way."

Traci joined in on the laughter.

"Shh, we don't want to wake your babies."

"No, we do not."

"How are my new niece and nephew?"

Traci wiped drool from Matthew's chin. "They're doing great. A double blessing from God."

"They sure are."

"How's the book signing? We're honored that you're our first in-house author."

"The honor is all mine. Thank goodness Mom and Dad could watch the kids. It's great to get some me time and so far, we've sold fifty copies of my book."

"Really?"

"Yes, indeed."

"It's because you're such a talented writer."

"I think it's because God is blessing our family beyond our wildest dreams."

"True."

A customer cleared her throat.

"I'm sorry. Go greet your adoring fans."

Gina resumed her job of meeting with customers and answering their questions about her book.

Marc approached, holding two cups from the café. Steam rose from the lids, carrying a delicious aroma. Caramel latte. He handed a cup to her and took a sip from his.

"Thank you."

"You're welcome, Mrs. Wonderful."

"I thought my last name was Roberts."

"It is, but I just wanted to you know what a blessing you are to me."

"You're a blessing to me too."

He sat beside her and leaned in, planting a tender kiss on her left cheek. "It's beautiful, isn't it?"

"More beautiful than I imagined."

She sent up a prayer of praise and gratitude to God. This was just the beginning of what God had in store for her family, her bookstore, and her life. She gazed at her still-sleeping babies, and her heart overflowed with joy. She wiped tears from her eyes. Crying was becoming as common to her as talking these days. Post-partum hormones.

Marc handed her a tissue and rubbed her middle back.

She was blessed to have him as her husband. She was blessed to be a mother to their babies, and most of all, she was blessed by God to be alive and experience this second chance. A second chance at love, a second chance at hope, a second chance to live her dreams.

$\sim$ THE END $\sim$

Author Bio: Alexis A. Goring is a writer at heart and a journalist by profession. She loves the art of storytelling and is especially delighted to have released her first book, an inspirational romance short story collection called *Hope in My Heart: A Collection of Heartwarming Stories*, in Sept. 2013.

She enjoys the interview process because it helps her to connect with people and learn life lessons from their personal stories. She loves to write news and feature stories for publication in newspapers and magazines. Blogging is a personal ministry for Alexis and she updates her "God is Love" blog on a weekly basis.

When she is not working on her next book, Alexis can be found listening to songs by her most admired musicians, enjoying the food in cafes/restaurants, shopping at her favorite malls and spending quality time with loved ones (family and friends).

She recently joined the Forget Me Not Romances family of traditionally published authors and is excited about the publication journey that God is taking her on.

Made in the USA
Middletown, DE
03 June 2017